RAELYN

A CHRISTIAN ROMANTIC SUSPENSE

OATH OF HONOR

LAURA SCOTT

PROLOGUE

Ten years earlier . . .

Isaiah Washington scanned the street for cops prior to approaching his drug contact, Petey Dobbs. Good thing the pigs didn't show up in this area very often. That made it easier to do business.

In this neighborhood, the Chief owned the streets. And the goal wasn't law and order but survival of the fittest.

"Yo," Petey said with a head bob. "Got what I need?"

"Got the cash?" Isaiah countered. Donte Wicks, his supplier, would want his money ASAP. The guy was as twitchy as the product he sold to those who lusted after it. Isaiah didn't much like being the middleman, but he hoped to have a face-to-face meeting with Donte's boss, the Chief, very soon. The more drugs he sold, the better his chances of moving up in the organization. This barely scrapping by was getting old.

One good thing about selling dope, it was good and easy money.

Considering he and his ma were one step away from living on the street, that's all he cared about. He eyed Petey

Dobbs warily. Petey was more skittish than usual. Isaiah wanted to make the sale and get out of there. Move on to the next job. With Donte, there was always another job waiting in the wings. And that was just fine with him.

"I'm a little short," Petey said, his gaze darting back and forth nervously. "But I'll get the rest by tomorrow. I promise."

"No cash, no deal." He was tired of Petey's games; this was the second time in a row the guy had tried to weasel out of paying. "Three hundred or nothing."

"Come on, Isa, you know I'm good for it," Petey whined. "My dad is out of town, but he'll be home later tonight. I promise I'll pay you in the morning."

Yeah, famous last words. Besides, he didn't believe him. No junky ever paid up after they'd scored their dope.

"No deal." Isaiah forced himself to turn away. There were others out there who would pay top dollar for what he had. He didn't need Petey as much as the idiot needed him. Finding a new buyer would take longer, though, and that delay would put Donte's undies in a wad. The guy had the patience of a cockroach.

"Okay, okay, wait!" Petey lunged forward to grab his arm.

Isaiah instantly reacted, lashing out with his fist, catching Petey in the jaw. He'd been robbed once before by a desperate junkie, and he wasn't about to go through that again.

Petey howled like a baby and let go of his arm. Isaiah took several steps backward, eyeing Petey cautiously. This was the second reason why he didn't like being the middle-man; these smackheads were unpredictable.

"Last chance." He should have left right away but had hoped Petey would hand over the cash.

Instead, the junkie whipped out a gun, pointed it at him, and pulled the trigger. The bullet slammed into his upper chest. The impact threw him off his feet, and he hit the ground hard, the back of his head bouncing off the pavement. Darkness hovered around the edges of his vision, but he did his best to stay conscious. He stared up in shock as Petey leaned over him and rummaged in his pockets for the drugs.

Then Petey was gone, leaving him lying in the street, unable to move. He looked up at the faint stars in the dark sky. Waves of pain washed over him, and he could feel his strength ebbing away, his blood pooling in the street.

This was it. He was gonna die out here like so many brothers who had gone before him. This was why his teachers had insisted that crime didn't pay. Anyone who lived in the hood knew that being shot was always a risk. Nothing he could do about that.

Desperate times called for desperate actions. His mom's illness, followed by losing her job, had started him down this path.

One that would end here tonight on a cold May evening.

His biggest regret was not getting the cash his ma would need to stay in their rattrap of an apartment for another month. She needed him. Needed the money he brought home every week.

But he'd failed her.

He closed his eyes, wishing death would take him quickly. Suddenly a blindingly white light filled his field of vision. Was this a dream? Isaiah squinted against the brightness because it hurt his eyes. Was that a spotlight? Had the cops arrived? Turning his head carefully, he looked around, realizing he was still alone. There was nothing other than the dazzling bright light.

A strange sense of peace washed over him as his grandmother's voice reverberated through his mind.

"Go to the light. Isaiah, you must go to the light!"

To the light? Was the light heaven? He found himself transfixed by the warm brightness. Yet he also didn't understand why the light would shine for someone like him. He lifted his arm as if to touch the light and experienced the odd sensation of his body being lifted off the street, drawn upward into the light's embrace.

Warmth enveloped him, and his heart filled with hope. *Yes! I need the light! Please, Lord, take me to the light!*

Just the thought of seeing his grandmother made him smile. But then another deeper voice in his mind whispered, "Not yet. It's not your time, my child."

Not yet? Or not ever? Isaiah closed his eyes, fearing the worst. That God had rejected him and was sending him straight to hell.

Where he belonged.

"Shots fired! Shots fired!" Lieutenant Joe Kingsley's voice was calm but tense in her earpiece. From her position at the abandoned warehouse, tactical police officer Raelyn Lewis could hear the shots easily enough. They sounded like firecrackers that might never stop. Her heart thudded painfully in her chest beneath her vest, but her hands didn't shake. She knew her job and was determined to execute it to the best of her ability.

She peeked out from behind the building to see what was happening. The situation outside the New Hope Church had spiraled out of control within seconds of the tactical team's arrival. The local police had gotten there first, and rather than dispersing, the group of kids had brandished their weapons and stood their ground.

It was like something out of a horror flick. Too many people with guns facing a slew of armed police officers. No way this would end well. The gunfire proved it.

More shots rang out, and even from here, she saw bodies crumpling to the ground. Not just those from the group of armed kids who'd started this mess, but there were at least three police officers down too.

Bad. This was really bad. The worst street riot she'd ever witnessed. And considering she'd grown up in a low-income housing project in Chicago, that was saying something. Chicago had a worse gun crime rate than Milwaukee, although you would never know it based on the scene unfolding today.

"We need to get the crowd under control," Joe said. "I want them surrounded. Jina, get in position."

"Roger that," Jina said.

"Moving in," Raelyn replied, agreeing with his command. The tactical team wasn't one for sitting around and watching. She quickly stepped out from behind the building. Her position near the abandoned warehouse happened to be closest to the church. Grayson was on the other side of the church, and several of her other teammates were stationed in other areas. Jina, their sharpshooter, was making her way to high ground as ordered, but Raelyn didn't know how long that would take.

There wasn't a second to spare. Keeping her head down and her rifle wedged up against her shoulder, she ran into the street. "Police! Drop your weapons! Now!"

At least five kids turned to see her heading toward them. Rather than dropping their weapons as ordered, one lifted his gun to fire at her. Thankfully, the bullet went high. She didn't hesitate to return fire, hitting him in the lower abdomen. The force of the bullet finding its mark had him dropping his weapon. She took aim at the next perp, but it seemed as if the reality of the situation had finally hit them because the four remaining kids turned and ran toward the church.

Oh no. She was not going to allow them to use the church as a hideout. Not when there was a half dozen bodies littering the street.

"Four perps, possibly armed, heading inside the church," she said into her mic as she broke into a run. "One down with a belly wound, he needs a bus." Her step faltered when she reached the young man she'd hit. He was lying on the ground sobbing in pain as he held his hands over the wound in his abdomen.

He didn't look a day older than sixteen.

"Apply pressure," she said, resisting the urge to kneel beside him. "Ambulance will be here soon." It wasn't easy to ignore his pleading eyes, but she didn't dare stop to provide aid. Those kids who'd run inside the church were likely armed, the way everyone in this disaster seemed to be. For all she knew, there were innocent people inside the church.

People who could be used as targets or hostages.

Covering the distance without delay, she swiftly mounted the three steps leading up to the main entrance. Keeping to the side, she drew the door open. Staying back, she listened intently and braced herself for the sound of gunfire.

Hearing nothing, she peeked around the corner. The interior of the church was dimly lit, making it difficult to see clearly. Easing around the doorway, she stepped farther into the church, still holding her weapon ready. She took one step up the center aisle, sweeping her gaze from left to right, then abruptly stopped when she saw one of the four boys who'd come inside, holding a mixed-race man dressed in a black shirt and slacks with a white collar around his throat at gunpoint.

"Stay back!" the kid shouted. "I'll cap him!"

"You don't want to do that," the dark-haired man said calmly. He was young, maybe her own age of thirty, and didn't appear the least bit alarmed. "Killing a man leaves a stain on your soul. God is watching over you."

"Shut up!" the kid shouted, looking nervously from side to side. Was he expecting backup from his friends? "You! Stay where you are, pig!"

Raelyn did as the kid demanded. She forced herself to sound reasonable. "Okay, I won't come any farther. You're the one calling the shots here. What's your name?"

"Drop the gun! Do it! I swear I'll shoot him!" The kid's wild eyes seemed to bore into her. Maybe he was on drugs, which would explain at least part of this debacle.

She didn't want to lower her weapon, but the serene and startling blue eyes of the pastor being held hostage gave her hope that he knew this kid. That even if the punk ran off, they'd be able to track him down later. "Okay. I hear you. I'm lowering my gun, see?" She made an exaggerated movement of pointing her weapon downward and then bending to set it on the floor. "No reason to shoot. Who are you? What's your name?"

"Shut up!" The kid's eyes were wild with fear and false bravado. If it wasn't for the handgun, which appeared to be a Glock, pressed firmly against the pastor's side, she'd have rushed him. The kid clearly hadn't thought this through. Now that he had the pastor as a hostage, he didn't seem to know what to do.

Time to help him out. She was the tactical team's second hostage negotiator. "What do you want?" Raelyn kept her voice soft and not threatening. "Money? A ride out of here? Just tell me what you need, and I can help you. I'll call my boss, and he'll bring us whatever you want."

"Money! Yeah, I want money!" The kid's eyes brightened. "I want a million dollars."

"I can get you money," she agreed, trying not to roll her eyes. "But you must know I can't get you a million dollars. There isn't a bank out there that has that much cash on hand." Typical teenager who didn't have a clue as to how the world worked. "How about a thousand dollars and a ride?"

The light in the teenager's eyes dimmed. Then suddenly a weariness crossed his features. "Forget it. You can't help me. No one can." The heavy note of despair in the teenager's voice hit like a sucker punch to the gut. He looked as if he'd lost everything. What on earth had happened out on the street? Before she could ask anything more, the kid deliberately turned the barrel of the gun toward her. Gut instinct had her hitting the floor seconds before the weapon reverberated in his hand. A bullet whizzed past her head. She kept moving, scooping the rifle up from the floor and rolling to her knees, bringing the barrel around to return fire.

"No!" The dark-haired man with blue eyes and light-caramel skin abruptly stepped into her line of fire.

"Move!" She glared at him with annoyance, then jumped to her feet and rushed past him toward the back of the church. But it was too late.

The armed kid was gone.

"WHAT IS WRONG WITH YOU?" The pretty cop whirled on him, anger sparking in her amber eyes. "Why did you let him get away?"

"He's just a kid." Isaiah did his best to remain calm,

although the sound of gunfire had taken him back to the night he'd almost died.

To the night he'd heard his grandmother's voice telling him to go to the light. Followed by God's voice telling him it wasn't his time.

"He fired at a police officer," she snapped. "I don't care if he's a kid. He attempted to shoot a cop. Not to mention holding you hostage and threatening to kill you."

He glanced at the name tag that identified her last name as Lewis. "He was scared. Can you blame him? They were surrounded by cops out there."

"Yeah, I can blame him." Officer Lewis stepped closer, getting right in his face. "He shouldn't have a gun or threaten to kill people. Especially a cop. And I should arrest you for aiding and abetting a criminal."

He nodded sagely. "You could do that. But those charges won't stick. By the way, we haven't met. I'm Pastor Isaiah Washington, and this is my church."

Her eyes widened briefly before narrowing again. "I don't care if you're the Pope, I'll toss your butt in jail."

"This isn't a Catholic church. We're a Christian nondenominational church, so all are welcome." Isaiah spread his hands. "Even you, Officer Lewis."

There was a flash of something he couldn't quite identify in her gaze, before she said, "Knock it off. I want that kid's name. And the names of the others who came inside with him. Right now!"

Isaiah slowly shook his head. "I'm afraid I can't give you that information."

"Can't or won't?" She took another threatening step toward him, her expression grim. "Do you understand how serious this is? There are injured or dead police officers outside, along with other dead civilians, many of them barely old enough to drive. I want the names of those kids who ran through here, or I will place you in handcuffs."

She had no way of knowing that this wouldn't be his first arrest. Granted, it had been ten years since he'd done time in jail. Yet she didn't really understand who he was or the role he played in this community. Over the years, he'd become a leader within the city, someone that people looked up to for hope. For guidance. For acceptance.

He'd answered God's call. Every day was a gift. One he intended to cherish.

Isaiah held her gaze. "You have every right to arrest me. I can't stop you. But you should know that the new mayor and his extended family all belong to this church, which is a sanctuary for those in need. Even those who may step across the line of the law. Trust me, I understand better than most the seriousness of this incident. The mayor is just as anxious to stop the violence in the city as you are. Hence the recent rejuvenation of this church."

"I highly doubt that the mayor cares more than I do about the violence in the streets," Officer Lewis said in a curt tone. "I'm the one risking my life out there every day. And those cops who were injured didn't ask to be shot and killed by a gang of ruthless kids either."

That was true. He understood the dilemma she faced; he didn't like thinking of the police officers and other innocent people who had lost their lives today. And the ironic part of this entire situation was that he'd made the call to bring the police here in the first place.

A decision that had blown up in his face.

Waves of despair threatened to overwhelm him. It seemed like every time he made a bit of progress, something like this slapped him back down. For months now, he'd been trying to do the right thing. There would be no end to the violent crime until the entire city cracked down on the illegal guns and drugs. He knew that better than most.

And that was exactly why he wouldn't give up. He would not ignore God's calling. After seeing the light and nearly dying on the street, he'd turned his life around. After getting out of jail, he had worked in a drug rehab facility as a peer counselor, then slowly integrated himself as an informal leader into the community. He preached about God's love, peace, and light. This church and his congregation—small as it might be—were important to him. And those kids who'd run through the place were young enough to be saved. Something he knew wouldn't happen if they were tossed in the system.

He held up his arms, placing his wrists together. "Go ahead and arrest me."

He'd assumed she was bluffing, but in a swift move, she'd slapped a pair of silver cuffs around his wrists. "Pastor Isaiah Washington, you're under arrest for aiding and abetting a criminal." Her gaze didn't waver as she went on to read him his rights. That, too, brought a flashback to when he'd been lying in a hospital with his ankle cuffed to the bed after undergoing surgery to repair the bullet wound in his chest. He'd been too doped up on pain meds to really appreciate his rights, but then again, it hadn't much mattered.

When she finished, she added, "Stay here." After gently pushing him toward one of the church pews, she walked away, speaking softly into a radio that was little more than an earpiece.

Despite the seriousness of the situation, he couldn't help smiling wryly at his predicament. He didn't think the DA's office would press charges against him, but then again, the insurrection that had taken place outside the church was horrifying in more ways than one. So much death and destruction. For what?

He lifted his gaze to the crucifix on the wall above the modest altar. If he was to spend more time in jail, so be it. He would take whatever punishment the legal system deemed fit. He could only hope and pray that he'd be set free sooner rather than later.

The pretty cop headed outside, no doubt bringing in reinforcements. He wasn't that concerned with being arrested. She was just trying to make a point.

Yet his job was to save lost souls.

A full ten minutes passed before Officer Lewis returned. He rose to his feet to meet her halfway. "I'm ready."

She scowled as if annoyed by his calm attitude. Her job wasn't easy either. And he could acknowledge that it was far more dangerous.

"The situation is under police control. Let's go." She tugged on his arm and drew him through the church and outside. The scene that greeted him nearly sent him to his knees. Several bodies were lying on the ground in pools of blood. So much like the way he had once been.

He froze, unable to move. To take another step. Had he caused this? Was this all his fault?

Lord, help me! Show me Your way!

"Pastor Washington?" Officer Lewis glared at him, her brow furrowed with suspicion. "What's wrong?"

He couldn't conjure the words to explain his role in the death and destruction he faced. He looked down at the ground, then dropped to his knees to pray.

Another crack of gunfire rang out. The pretty cop threw herself on top of him, slamming him face down on the concrete steps as the area erupted into chaos.

"More shots fired!" someone shouted.

Stunned, he tried to lift his head, but Officer Lewis continued to hold him down. And that's when he realized that for the second time in his life, someone had just tried to kill him.

CHAPTER TWO

"Shooter is at the abandoned warehouse," Jina said into her earpiece. "I've pinned him down but need a team to investigate."

"On it," Roscoe drawled in his Texas accent. He and Zeke took off running toward the abandoned warehouse she'd recently used as cover. Had the gunman been in there the whole time? If so, why not take her out when he'd had the chance?

No, it wasn't likely the guy had been inside the warehouse the entire time. He would have taken the opportunity to pick off a few more cops. Instead, he'd fired at the pastor. What was that about?

"Let me up," Isaiah said with a grunt.

"Stay down." What part of being used for target practice didn't he understand? "We're searching for the shooter."

"Raelyn! Are you both okay?" Joe and Grayson came running toward her, crouching on either side of them.

"We're fine." She raised her head enough to glance over their shoulders. "No other shooters in the area?"

"We just finished clearing the area," Joe said grimly. "Or so we thought."

"The shooter could have sneaked into the warehouse at any point," she said. "I'm sure if he'd been in there the whole time, he'd have fired at me when I ran past."

"Maybe, but I still don't like it," Joe muttered.

"Can I please get up now?" Isaiah Washington asked.

"Not yet." She didn't move off him. Roscoe and Zeke had disappeared inside the warehouse, and it was suddenly eerily quiet. Seconds ticked by with excruciating slowness.

Finally, she heard Jina's voice through her earpiece. "The guys have cleared it. Repeat, the warehouse is clear."

That was both a relief and incredibly frustrating. How had the shooter gotten away? She knew it hadn't taken that long for Roscoe and Zeke to head over. They should have been quick enough to catch the gunman.

"Let's get him back inside the church," Grayson said tersely, gesturing at Isaiah. "One cop dead on the scene is bad enough."

"Only one? I thought I saw three down." She levered herself up and off the pastor.

"Two critically injured and on their way to Trinity Medical Center," Joe confirmed.

She shook her head, knowing there were several dead teens too. What a mess. "Pastor Washington? You can get up now." She stepped back to give him room. "But stay close. We're heading back inside the church."

"Thank you." Isaiah didn't argue. When he managed to stand, she felt a little guilty when she saw her handcuffs were still around his wrists. Swallowing a sigh, she escorted him inside the church and over to the pew.

Then she reached for the key to release the cuffs.

"I'm not under arrest anymore?" He appeared surprised by her action.

Frankly, she was surprised by her decision too. "I should take you in, but we need to understand what just happened out there. Starting with who tried to kill you."

Isaiah glanced up at her, his expression dazed. "I have no idea."

"You seriously expect me to believe that?" She was getting mighty tired of his stubborn attitude. "Okay, let's go through this again. First a bunch of kids with guns gather outside your church. Then you protect an armed teenager who held you hostage and took a shot at me, and now you claim you have no idea who just tried to kill you."

He flushed and nodded. "I agree the situation doesn't look good. I understand your concern. And the boy was scared, that's all. I don't think he really tried to hit you."

"I'm not *concerned*," she said in a low voice. "I'm angry. People died here today. You and I were almost killed too. Quit playing games. What gives?"

From the corner of her eye, she noticed Joe and Grayson were watching them warily. She did her best to ignore them.

"Okay. You're right about one thing," Isaiah said with a grimace. "I am partly responsible."

Now they were getting somewhere. She softened her tone. "What happened?"

He stared down at his hands for a moment, then lifted his gaze to hers. "I noticed a group of kids outside the church buying and selling drugs. I called an anonymous tip to the third district police station to let them know. I did not give them my name, but I did mention I saw at least one weapon."

She was shocked by his candor. "You said you were in your office working when the shots were fired."

"I was." He closed his eyes for a moment as if he couldn't bear to remember. "I know what you're thinking. It wasn't me being a coward, because I walk with God and am not afraid to die." He lifted his hand to rub his upper chest in a seemingly unconscious gesture. "I was only hoping to keep my involvement anonymous mainly because I need this church to be a refuge for those who seek peace and safety." He paused, then added, "But I wasn't about to ignore a major drug deal going down either."

"So that kid who held you hostage was one of the drug dealers?"

"No, he wasn't the one involved with the drugs, not at first." Isaiah's brow furrowed. "I'm not sure when he arrived on the scene."

"I still need his name." She would bet money on the Glock matching the bullets found at the scene outside.

"I told you before, I don't know his name." There was something about the way he responded that indicated he knew more than he was letting on.

"Look, Preach, you better start cooperating, or I'll slap those cuffs back on and haul you downtown."

"My name is Isaiah." He sighed and rubbed his jaw. "I don't know his legal name. But I've heard his street name."

"I'll take whatever information you have." She tried not to show her annoyance with the way he was splitting hairs. He must have known the kid's street name earlier, too, but hadn't seen fit to tell her. Not even when she'd clapped handcuffs around his wrists.

Before he could tell her anything more, Joe crossed over. He drew her from Isaiah so they could speak freely. "We need to go outside and talk to the district three captain and two detectives who just showed up."

She hesitated, glancing back at Isaiah. "Not sure we

should leave him here after the way someone tried to kill him. At least not until the scene has been cleared."

Joe frowned. "Yeah, okay. You stay close. Grayson and I will head outside."

"Wait." She didn't like being stuck on babysitting duty. "We can get one of the officers outside to sit on him."

"Not happening. Three of their own were shot, one dead and two injured. They're taking the lead on the investigation." Joe shrugged. "Rhy just wants us to offer assistance as needed until the area is completely cleared. He's not putting us on modified duty either." Joe pinned her with a gaze. "I know you hit one teen, and Roscoe did too. You'll have to give your gun to the detectives, but you'll be allowed to use a backup piece."

"Okay." She could tell there was no point in arguing. She was relieved Rhy wasn't taking them off the street, even though she knew that was the usual protocol. And she could understand the decision to allow district three officers to take the lead. If one of the casualties had been a member of their tactical team, there wouldn't be a cop on the planet who could keep them away. "Let me know if you need anything."

"Will do." Joe cut a glance toward Isaiah. "Go easy on him. He's trying to do a good thing here. This neighborhood needs a church."

She nodded without saying anything. She understood where Joe was coming from. He was a man of God too. A believer like Steele, Brock, and their boss, Captain Rhy Finnegan.

But not her.

After the guys left, she turned back to Isaiah. He wasn't in the pew where she'd left him. He was walking up the side of the church toward the altar.

"Isaiah? Hold on, we're not finished yet." She hurried after him, her gaze taking in the crucifix hanging above the simple table covered in a white cloth. He'd mentioned this was a Christian nondenominational church. She wondered what that meant. Then she told herself it didn't matter.

He led the way into his office. She hovered in the doorway, noticing the tall bookshelf behind him full of different books and a few Bibles. Why more than one? She had no clue.

"Officer Lewis," he said with a nod. "Please take a seat."

So formal, she thought as she dropped into the plain hard-backed chair. "I know you care about the law and justice," she said. "Or you wouldn't have made that call to the district three police station about the drug deal. So why are you harboring a cop killer?"

"You don't know that boy killed anyone," he protested.

"We have one dead cop and two critically injured," she said in a clipped tone. "And I have reason to believe that kid fired at one of them."

Isaiah frowned, then slowly nodded. "I see. Because of the way he said no one could help him now."

"Exactly." She held his gaze. "If you ask me, that was pretty much a confession. I understand you want the church to be a sanctuary, but that doesn't excuse harboring a cop killer."

"You don't know he killed an officer, and I'm not harboring him." Isaiah spread his hands wide. "He's not here in the church."

She ground her teeth together. "This is serious. I need to find this kid. Are you really going to refuse to help me?"

Isaiah dropped his gaze to the desk. It was all she could do not to leap across, grab him by the shoulders, and shake him. After what seemed like eons, he lifted his gaze. "He goes by his street name, Pinky."

"Pinky?" Was he for real? "Why Pinky?"

"Because he lost the pinky finger of his right hand when his father smashed it with a hammer," Isaiah said, his blue eyes dark with pain.

She could only stare at him in horrified shock, feeling his anguish. The explanation was awful. Even though she was no stranger to growing up poor and in an abusive household, the image of some man smashing his son's finger with a hammer made her sick to her stomach. "Was his father arrested?"

"No, because Pinky's mother told the police his finger was slammed in a car door. Even though they didn't have a car." He sighed. "Don't you see? These kids aren't born bad. They're products of their environment."

"That may be so." She was a product of her environment, too, wasn't she? But she'd taken a different path, escaping the lure of easy money in the streets. Besides, having compassion for the kid's situation didn't extend to ignoring the law. "I still need that weapon to see if it matches the slugs that will be taken out of these fallen officers. They deserve justice."

"I understand. But even if you find Pinky and the Glock, you don't know for sure he was the one to fire at those officers." Isaiah shrugged. "He may have picked up the gun from the ground."

What, he was a cop now? She frowned. "I thought you didn't see anything?"

"I didn't." He looked tired and sick over the violence that had erupted just yards from his church. She couldn't help a flash of sympathy. For someone who did believe, this situation couldn't be easy. "I'm just saying that the fact that

Pinky had the gun in his hand doesn't mean he fired at one of your fellow officers."

Isaiah seemed determined to protect this kid at all costs. And she could understand, to a point. "It would be easier to believe that theory if he hadn't taken a shot at me before bolting out of here." When he opened his mouth to argue, she quickly added, "But I will keep that possibility in mind once I find him."

Isaiah's expression was grim. "I hope you do."

Why did she feel as if she were one of the bad guys? She and the rest of their tactical team put their lives on the line every day for their community. She didn't appreciate him trying to make her feel as if she was part of the problem. "Is there anything else you can tell me? Like additional street names for the other kids who ran through here?"

He frowned, then leaned forward to grab a pen. He jotted down a short list of four names. "These are the only ones I know, and that's only because they've attended church services." A crooked smile tugged at the corner of his mouth. "The kids talk to each other freely as if I'm invisible."

She was surprised to hear they'd bothered to attend services but stayed focused on the list. "Congo, Dagger, Tiger, and Snoop?"

"Yes." He didn't elaborate.

It was like pulling teeth. "Do you know the stories behind all of their nicknames?" She pressed.

"Congo used to play the drums. Dagger is skinny and is known to carry a knife, and Tiger has a large orange Afro as he is also a mixed-race child. I'm not sure about Snoop."

She made those additional notes, then stood. "Thanks for this." Her main priority was to find Pinky and his Glock.

Then she remembered how she hadn't wanted to leave him alone. "I'll see if we can arrange for more police protection."

"No need. I'll be fine." He didn't look concerned. "Pinky didn't want to kill me."

"Someone did." She considered calling Joe, but then she decided against it. The pastor should be safe enough in church. Getting these kids into custody had to be a priority. And now that she had names and even a description, she was anxious to get started. "Your choice to stay here or have an officer escort you home. I'll see you later, then."

As she turned away, Isaiah called out to her. "Officer Lewis?"

She paused to glance over her shoulder. "Yeah?"

"I pray you find the peace you're seeking." He smiled gently, and she was surprised at how handsome he looked. "God is always there, waiting for you. You and your teammates are welcome to our Sunday service any time."

Don't hold your breath. Somehow, she managed not to say the words that flashed in her mind. Instead, she simply nodded and left.

After seeing the death and destruction that had just transpired outside the church, she didn't understand how anyone, even Isaiah, could believe in God.

ISAIAH TOLD himself not to feel guilty for giving Raelyn the information about the kids' street names. The truth was, the situation that had unraveled outside couldn't happen again, and if that meant some of these kids doing time in a juvie center, then so be it.

Yet he wasn't sure Raelyn—*Officer Lewis*, he swiftly

corrected himself—would agree with his assessment of where they should be held if found guilty of a crime.

It was no secret they were on opposite sides here. Not that he condoned violence in any way. No one should be fired upon, much less police officers. But he also knew what these kids dealt with every day. They didn't have easy lives.

But they did have choices. And many of them had made the wrong ones today.

The way he once had. He absently rubbed the scar on his chest through his black shirt. God had saved him for a reason. To be here today. To help these kids in any way possible. And logically, he knew that didn't include protecting criminals.

Yet he still didn't believe Pinky was responsible for killing a cop. Of the group of boys who'd attended services, Congo was the most hardened of the group. Isaiah offered a free meal after his Sunday service, which was the main reason Pinky and the other kids had come in the first place. Isaiah had known the kids had probably just wanted to escape their home situations for a while, but he had hoped maybe his message of God and faith was getting through.

Now this. He dropped his head into his hands. Even though he was a pastor and knew God had spared his life, and that Jesus had died for his sins, it wasn't easy to simply accept God's plan. Not when things like a massive shoot-out in broad daylight occurred.

Not when so many had been killed or injured.

He tried not to wallow in despair.

Please, Lord Jesus, protect Your children. Please keep them safe from harm. Amen.

Normally, he felt better after praying. But not tonight. He forced himself to work on his sermon for the upcoming

Sunday. Rather than focusing on forgiveness, he needed to discuss God's Ten Commandments.

Thou shalt not kill.

No, that might be too preachy. He wrote and rewrote for what seemed like hours before giving up. Pushing the tablet of paper aside, he rose to his feet. Something would come to him. It always did.

Making his way through the church, he opened the front door. The voices outside had stopped a while ago, and he was surprised to see the street outside his church was deserted. He must have worked longer than he'd realized.

He was troubled to see the blood stains on the ground along with the remnants of crime scene tape strung across the area.

How many children had lost their lives today?

And how many more would be lost if they didn't get the violence in the city under control?

With a heavy sigh, he turned and locked the church door. He didn't like locking the church, but he didn't have a choice. Not after the drug deal and subsequent shooting. He then walked down the few steps to street level. Glancing around, he noticed the homes across the street had their curtains drawn tightly over the windows. Those who may have been involved in what happened today and had escaped—like Pinky—would likely hunker down and stay out of sight for the next few days.

A good thing, he thought, as the neighborhood and city in general needed time to recover from this. He should have asked Officer Lewis to get him the names of the children who'd lost their lives. He needed to visit with their families, offer to have funeral services at the church for them.

It wouldn't be enough, and it may not even welcomed,

but he would try anyway. Because that was his role here. To help pick up the pieces after a terrible tragedy.

Despite how someone had taken a shot at him earlier, he decided to work a few hours providing rideshares to earn enough to cover the next after-service meal. Most people didn't realize he worked a part-time job in addition to his role as pastor, but that was okay. He hadn't taken the role as pastor for the money. A church in this neighborhood could never exist solely on donations.

He barely made enough in donations to pay the monthly electric, heat, and water bills. And that was with the mayor's unwavering support.

Lifting his face into the cool May breeze coming in off the lake, he turned toward home, walking the five blocks to the house the mayor rented to him for a ridiculously low rate. He'd often wondered if the mayor had done that because he and Beau, the mayor's son, had attended the same high school.

Ten years ago, after he'd gotten out of the hospital, and after his stint in jail, he'd discovered his mother had died after another round of pneumonia. Her health had never been very good; she'd always suffered more acutely from colds or the flu than others. The doctors had mentioned she had a weakened immune system. At first, he'd been angry at learning of her death, wondering why God had saved him over his mother.

Then he remembered the bright, welcoming light. The whispered words from his grandmother, urging him to go to the light. He believed his mother was in heaven with his grandmother, free of pain and suffering.

His turn was coming, he knew. It had nearly happened today if not for Raelyn—Officer Lewis's quick reaction. His future was in God's hands.

When he reached the house, he slid in behind the wheel of his car and logged into the app that would allow him to take fares as a rideshare driver. He dug the decals out of his pocket and stuck them to the windshield. Then he headed out toward the nicer part of town, where people could afford to pay for rideshares to get from one place to the other.

He drove steadily for the next four hours, doing relatively well considering the day he'd had. Most of the people he picked up and dropped off ignored him, other than making sure he had the address of where they wanted to go. And that was fine with him. He didn't care for small talk and would rather focus on driving. It was interesting, though, how many people discussed their personal lives, as if he couldn't hear every word.

Being both a pastor and a rideshare driver seemed to make him invisible.

His thoughts went back to the crack of gunfire that had Raelyn tackling him to the ground. He hadn't been lying when he said he had no idea who wanted to kill him. Unless he was wrong about Pinky. And the other kids?

No, he couldn't believe any of those kids were hard-core killers. Not yet anyway. In time, if things didn't change for them, they could easily turn into killers. Congo had hard eyes, so he wasn't sure whether Congo could be drawn back from the edge. But the others? They were young and scared, and he felt certain the cops hanging around outside would have ensured they stayed far away.

Besides, why would they kill him? He'd only offered support, food, and comfort.

He glanced at his watch. It was almost midnight. He usually stopped working at this time of night because there was generally a lull between midnight and bar time. And he didn't particularly care for driving intoxicated people around. Not only were they rude and bad tippers, but on two separate occasions, drunk passengers had thrown up in the back seat of his car.

Nope. Not doing that again.

He decided to pick up one last fare, then head home. The three girls he'd picked up to drive back to their dorm at Marquette University were nice enough. And he was glad to get them home safely. That was the part of the job he liked.

Returning to his neighborhood was like going from earth to the moon. It was depressing how these families lived in poverty. Broken-down homes and cars. Boarded-up windows on businesses that had failed. He pulled into the driveway of the rental house and threw the gearshift into park. Sliding out from behind the wheel, he hit the key fob to lock the door.

As he turned to head up the short sidewalk to his front door, he hesitated, realizing his porch light was out. A burned bulb? He'd never changed it during the time he'd stayed here, so it was entirely possible.

Yet living on these streets brought his guard up. Moving slowly, he approached his porch. Seeing nothing amiss, he relaxed. He was letting the events of the day wreak havoc on his imagination.

But he'd only taken one step up when a large Black man lunged from the side of the house, roughly knocking him to the ground.

Isaiah hit the earth hard. The darkness made it impossible to see the attacker's features clearly, other than the dark color of his skin and the whiteness of his eyes. He tried to strike back, but the large Black man's hands wrapped around his throat.

"You deserve this," a voice rasped near his ear.

He did? Isaiah struggled to peel the steely fingers away from his throat. Maybe he deserved to die, but what about his mission?

What about the kids he was supposed to save?

Isaiah expected to see the light again, but there was nothing but darkness. Had God given up on him?

"Stop! Police!" a familiar female voice shouted.

Instantly, the big Black man let him go and surged to his feet. As Isaiah gasped for air, his assailant kicked him once in the ribs, then took off running. A minute later, Raelyn shot past Isaiah lying on the ground in hot pursuit.

Forcing himself to his feet, he winced at his sore ribs and followed Raelyn. He didn't know if the large Black man was armed or not, but he was afraid for Raelyn's safety if he was carrying.

Was this guy the same one who'd tried to shoot him earlier? Isaiah stumbled, struggling to stay upright. His chest felt tight, and he sucked air into his lungs as he forced himself to keep going, even though he was already lagging behind.

Then finally, Raelyn slowed to a stop. She turned, and he could see that she was speaking into her radio. "This is unit ten requesting backup in pursuing a perp." She glanced at him and began walking toward him. "Assailant is an African American man roughly six feet three inches tall, three hundred pounds and was last seen heading north on Clover. He's wanted for the assault and attempted murder of Pastor Isaiah Washington."

Then she lowered her hand and raked her gaze over him. "Are you okay? Do you need an ambulance?"

"No ambulance. Sore throat and ribs, that's all." His voice was hoarse, and he feared the tissues might continue to swell due to the assailant's tight grip. Pain sliced through his side, but he wasn't going to complain.

"Let's get back to your place." She fell into step beside him.

It didn't take long for them to reach his house. He turned to face her. "Why did you come to my place tonight?"

"I was afraid something like this would happen." She paused, then added, "Who was that man?"

"I don't know."

She threw up her hands in a theatrical gesture. "Here we go again. You honestly have never seen that man before in your life. You don't know who that man was or why he attacked you?"

"I swear I don't." He tried to think back to those moments the large Black man had him pinned on the ground but couldn't place the brief glimpse he'd gotten of his face with anyone who'd attended his church services. "He said I deserved it."

"He said that?" she demanded. "Those were his exact words?"

"Yes." He continued up the steps to his front door, putting his key in the lock and heading inside for an ice pack.

Dazed at the realization that the threat against his life was real. Not just a fluke shot outside the church, but a desperate attempt to kill him.

And whoever wanted him dead would keep coming after him until the deed was done.

CHAPTER THREE

Raelyn did her best to rein in her frustration. Maybe the pastor didn't recognize the guy who'd attacked him, but it seemed as if he was determined to protect the people of this neighborhood more so than getting the assailant behind bars. "I need to take a formal statement." She glanced at his car, then back at him. "Where were you tonight?"

Isaiah gestured to the house. "Please come inside where we can speak privately."

"Fine." She had to admit it was probably safer to have him off the street. She glanced around as she followed him up to the small porch. There was no sign of the perp, of course, but that didn't mean others weren't hiding nearby.

This was the second time in a matter of hours that someone had tried to kill him, and she wanted to know who they were and why they were targeting him.

"Would you like something to drink? Coffee? Water? Soft drink?"

"No thanks." She was exhausted but didn't think coffee this late was a good idea. She'd been back to the precinct to get her backup weapon. It was a replica of her regular service weapon, which was nice. She still had a third gun that she sometimes used off duty, but a small weapon tucked in an ankle holster wasn't as convenient.

"Please excuse me while I grab an ice pack for my throat." He disappeared into the kitchen where she could hear him rummaging in the freezer.

She was impressed at how neat and tidy the place was. The furniture was worn but sturdy. The carpet also showed signs of wear, but it had also been recently vacuumed, and there wasn't any dust that she could see.

In truth, Pastor Washington was a better housekeeper than she was. Or maybe someone from the church cleaned for him. He was handsome enough that she imagined the single women in the area would be throwing themselves at him.

"Please sit down." He gestured to the sofa and dropped into the overstuffed chair nearby. He pressed a bag of frozen corn to his throat. "I appreciate your help again, Officer Lewis. If you hadn't been there . . ." He didn't finish.

"Call me Raelyn. All this pastor and officer stuff is a bit much."

"Of course. And please call me Isaiah." He smiled again, despite the recent attack.

"I'm glad I was able to help." She frowned at the frozen corn. "Are you sure you don't want to go to the hospital to have your throat looked at?"

"I'm sure." His blue gaze was calm, as if this wasn't the first time he'd been attacked. And really, what did she know about him? There hadn't been time to dig into Isaiah Washington's past. She and Grayson had spent hours trying to find Pinky, to no avail. Then she had done another two hours of paperwork before she'd come back here.

Just in time to save Isaiah's life.

"Your choice." She couldn't force him to get treatment. "But I still need to know where you were this evening." It suddenly occurred to her that Isaiah may have been hiding Pinky here for the past few hours.

"I'm a rideshare driver." Isaiah's statement surprised her. Then, as if reading her mind, he added, "I can prove that by showing you my list of fares for the past four and a half hours if necessary."

"Rideshare driver," she repeated. "I thought you were the church pastor?"

"The two roles are not mutually exclusive." He offered a lopsided smile. "My job as church pastor fulfills my heart and my sense of purpose. Being a rideshare driver fills my bank account and allows me to provide community meals after each Sunday service."

"I see." She sat back on the sofa, realizing she may have misjudged him. Although he was still protecting those kids. "Back to the attack, you're sure you didn't recognize that man? He must know you if he said you deserved it."

"I didn't get a close look at him." Isaiah grimaced. "He caught me off guard, slamming me to the ground, then strangling me. It was dark because my porch light was out. Maybe he did that, I don't know. Regardless, you probably got a better look at him than I did."

"I wish I had, but I was in your backyard when I heard the scuffle. By the time I ran around the corner, all I could see was his back as he attempted to strangle you." She sighed. "Then he took off. I never got a good look at his face."

He shifted the cold back onto his throat. "You think he's the same one who took a shot at me outside the church?"

"Yes, unless you have more than one person who wants you dead." She leaned forward, propping her elbows on her knees. "You mentioned calling in the drug deal going down outside the church. You didn't give your name, but I'm thinking whoever attacked you knew you made that anonymous call. And they're striking back in revenge."

He looked thoughtful for a moment. "That's possible. But if that was the case, I would expect to be issued a warning rather than being killed outright."

"A warning?" she scoffed. "In this neighborhood? Doubtful."

He shrugged. "I just can't imagine being killed for a call that I may or may not have made. The neighbors across the street could have just as easily contacted the police. Not everyone living here condones crime."

She hated to admit that much was true. The police had gotten various stories from the few witnesses who had stayed indoors. But two people in those homes directly across from the three dead kids told the exact same story. They both described how two squads carrying four officers arrived to break up the gathering. The situation escalated, and one of the officers fired first, shooting and killing a teenager. That's when several other kids pulled weapons and fired back.

"We talked to those neighbors. They saw the police arrive on the scene and informed us they fired the first shot." She hadn't liked hearing that, but then again, so many of the kids were armed, so she couldn't blame the officers for doing whatever was necessary to break things up. "But you didn't see that, right?"

"Correct." He frowned. "I wish I had. I feel responsible since I'm the one who made that phone call."

"You did the right thing." She softened her tone. Normally, she was easygoing, but there was something about Isaiah that riled her up. "Deaths from drug overdoses are on the rise. It's not good that kids are dealing drugs."

He winced and nodded. She eyed him curiously. She got the feeling he was holding back on her. Again.

"Have you seen Pinky since he left the church?" she asked.

"No. I haven't seen anyone from the incident. As I already told you, I worked late, then headed out to do my rideshare hours." He seemed annoyed now. "Is there anything else? I could use some sleep."

She shrugged and rose to her feet. "That's all for now. However, you really need to be careful. Whoever that guy was, he obviously knows where you live and where you work. I don't think it's a stretch to believe he'll try again."

If she thought Isaiah would look frightened by that prospect, she was wrong. He simply nodded, set the bag of corn aside, and stood. "I understand. I will make sure to lock up after you leave."

She hesitated, wondering if leaving him here alone was the right thing to do. She didn't want anything to happen to him, but it wasn't as if the Milwaukee Police Department had the budget to pay for a cop to sit outside his house all night either.

Shaking off the thought, she strode to the front door. Then she abruptly turned and took a business card from her pocket. "This is my personal cell number. If someone shows up here, you need to call 911, but if you remember something or hear from Pinky, I respectfully ask you to call me."

He took the card, looking down at it for a moment. "I will. Thanks again, Raelyn."

Hearing her name in his low husky voice made her tummy do a little flip. She ignored it. "Be safe, Isaiah." She walked out into the cool night, waiting for him to close and lock the door behind her.

She'd left her squad on the next block over. Technically, she was off duty and shouldn't be dressed in her full uniform or driving the squad. But since she'd gotten here in time to interrupt the attack, she doubted Joe or Rhy would give her any grief over it.

After sliding in behind the wheel, she started the car and thought about the large Black man who'd tried to strangle Isaiah. The first attempt had been a long-distance shot, and this more recent attempt had been up close and personal.

Two different perps? Maybe.

Her intent had been to head to her small home, but instead, she found herself driving around the block and pulling up in front of Isaiah's house. She sat for a moment, the engine idling, wondering if she should call Joe or Rhy to ask about offering the pastor protection.

As he wasn't a material witness, she couldn't imagine how they'd justify the expense. Then she thought about Isaiah taking rideshares to make ends meet. To offer meals for those who attended church.

With a resigned sigh, she shut down the engine and hunkered down in the front seat. She'd stick around for a while, just in case. Only because she didn't want the pastor's death on her conscience. She didn't believe in God, but she'd seen enough to know there were plenty of devils walking among them.

Like Pinky's father. And Kenny, her mother's boyfriend who'd attempted to rape her when she was only thirteen.

Oh yeah. The devils walked among them often in plain sight. And her job was to protect and serve, keeping evil at bay.

ISAIAH DIDN'T SLEEP WELL, partially because of the pain in his ribs and his sore throat, but mostly because of the events that had transpired during the day. He kept seeing Pinky's panicked gaze in his mind, only he was cuffed and helpless to ease the child's pain.

He dragged himself up at six o'clock the following morning, stumbling toward the kitchen. As he moved past the living room, the sight of a squad parked out front brought him up short.

What in the world?

Wide awake now, he detoured from his quest to get coffee and crossed the living room. Without hesitation, he yanked open the front door and headed outside.

To his surprise, Raelyn slid out from behind the wheel. He stopped abruptly, conscious of his flannel pants, T-shirt, and slippers. "Have you been out here all night?"

She yawned. "Yeah. I don't suppose you have any coffee?"

"I was just going to make a pot." He gestured for her to come inside. "I'll cook breakfast too."

She followed him into the house. Hard to imagine she'd gotten any rest dressed in uniform and sitting in a squad all night. He felt guilty even though he hadn't asked her to do that. He quickly crossed to the counter to get the coffee going.

"You'll be glad to know everything was quiet last night," she said, dropping into a kitchen chair.

"No surprise, I'm sure your squad scared everyone off," he said with a smile.

"I thought Pinky might show up or the big Black guy, but the streets were empty." She yawned again, then scrubbed her hands over her face. "Do you mind if I borrow your bathroom?"

"Of course, first door on the right."

"Thanks." She headed that way.

He decided to take the opportunity to change into real clothes, choosing jeans and a long-sleeved T-shirt. Feeling better, he returned to the kitchen to begin breakfast.

Feeding her seemed like the least he could do. He had just a few eggs left and some toast. Hopefully, that would be enough to pay her back for staying up all night to watch over him. Oh, he understood she'd only stayed to catch Pinky or his assailant, but he still appreciated her dedication to her job.

It is about the only thing we have in common, he thought with a wry smile.

When Raelyn returned a few minutes later, her hair was down, and she looked more relaxed. "That coffee smells good."

"Have a seat." He quickly set the nearly empty carton of eggs aside to reach for a mug. "Black? Or cream and sugar?"

"Black." She frowned. "You don't need to cook for me. I just wanted some coffee before heading home."

"You don't like eggs and toast?" He handed her the mug of coffee. "I have enough for both of us."

She hesitated, cradling the mug, then nodded. "I like eggs and toast. If you're sure it's no trouble."

"It's not." He quickly went to work, feeling somewhat nervous having her there. After living alone for so many years, he wasn't accustomed to entertaining.

His short stint in jail had given him a deep appreciation for privacy. Having a place to stay and a job that helped put food on the table among other things was a gift. One he didn't take for granted.

"I hope you don't have to work today." He glanced at her over his shoulder. "You need time to sleep."

"I'm not scheduled to work until three p.m." She yawned again, then took another sip of her coffee. "Plenty of time to get a few hours of rack time in."

He didn't like it. Shouldn't cops be well rested before heading out to the street? But he kept his thoughts to himself, unwilling to upset the hint of camaraderie between them.

"Scrambled, sunny-side up, or over easy?" He held two eggs in his hand.

"Whatever you're having is fine." She shrugged. "Scrambled isn't bad when they're real eggs rather than the powdered stuff you get in the army."

"Ah, that explains the phrase 'rack time,'" he said. "How long did you serve in the military?"

"Four years." She tilted her head to the side. "Long enough to grow up and decide it was better to risk my life keeping the peace here at home rather than in a foreign country halfway across the globe."

He should have guessed she'd served time in the armed forces. Raelyn might look like a beauty queen, but she was tough as nails and not afraid to wade into danger. The way she'd tried to talk Pinky into giving up his weapon had been impressive.

"Over easy it is," he said lightly. "But don't yell at me if I break your yolks."

"Yell about eggs?" She shook her head. "Not likely. Now if you were harboring Pinky in here, there might be something to yell about."

"I'm not." He supposed he couldn't blame her for believing the worst.

"But you would if you could," she said.

He put bread in the toaster, then turned to face her. "Pinky is barely fifteen. He's young and needs support and guidance, not jail." When she opened her mouth to argue, he lifted his hand. "I know he shot at you. I know he shouldn't have a gun. I know he broke the law. But maybe he's better off in a juvenile detention facility rather than jail."

She eyed him over the rim of her mug. "You think juvie is that much better?"

"I don't know, I never spent time there." But he had spent time in jail and had to believe a juvenile facility was better for Pinky. "At least think about it."

She didn't respond for a long moment. "You sound as if you know what it's like to be locked up."

He was surprised she hadn't looked up his criminal background already. Although she had been busy saving his life, searching for Pinky and the others, then saving his life again. "I do. Did a year and a half in the house of corrections when I was eighteen."

"For what?" She didn't look as if she were judging him, but that she was genuinely interested. Maybe she needed to hear his story. To know that where there was God, there was hope. Even for Pinky.

"Dealing drugs." He lifted his hand to rub his chest. "Unfortunately, a guy who didn't have enough cash on him for the deal decided to shoot me to get the dope."

She sucked in a harsh breath, looking horrified. "You were shot? In the chest?"

"Yes." He eyed the eggs in the pan, then turned to her. "That was ten years ago, and I admit I made bad choices that almost got me killed. My mom was sick and lost her job as a housekeeper at the hospital. Dealing drugs was easy money." He shook his head and sighed. "Until it wasn't."

"I'm sorry, that sounds rough." She propped her elbows on the table. "But you turned your life around. Made another choice to change your path."

"Yes. Because I saw the light." The toast popped, and he quickly buttered the bread, then flipped the eggs. A minute later, he brought their plates to the table. "I would like to say grace."

"Ah, sure." She bowed her head, holding her hands in her lap.

"Dear Lord, we thank You for this food we are blessed to eat. We ask that You continue to keep all Your children safe in Your care. Amen."

"Amen," she added, after a slight hesitation. Then she reached for her fork. "Thanks. This looks delicious."

"You're welcome." He took a bite of his toast, trying to think of something to say that would help her accept God's presence. He'd had the benefit of almost dying to learn about God, but obviously he didn't want Raelyn to go through something like that.

For a pastor, he wasn't very good at this.

"You said it's been ten years since you were a drug dealer," she said, interrupting his thoughts. "You must have known the players back then."

"I only knew the handful I dealt with," he said. "It's not as if those on the lower levels of the drug-running organization knows who's at the top of the chain."

She narrowed her gaze. "There you go again, protecting criminals."

"I'm not." He sighed, then added, "I highly doubt the same players are hanging around all this time later." He thought for a minute about Donte Wicks. He'd been tall, but not heavy like his assailant. Donte had been a hundred and fifty pounds soaking wet. Besides, the last time he'd checked, and that was only a few weeks ago, Donte was still in jail.

But that made him wonder how Donte had gotten arrested. Had he been caught? Despite nearly dying, he'd never told the police about Donte Wicks. First because he'd been on a bunch of meds after having surgery and later because they hadn't asked.

"Maybe not, but I think it's second nature for you to protect those living in your neighborhood," she said. "You can't save them all, Isaiah. The man who assaulted you is still out there."

"I know." Of course, he couldn't save them all. But he could save one or two at a time. And that was worth it.

They ate in silence for a few minutes. When they were finished, he carried their empty plates to the sink. "More coffee?"

"No thanks. I need to get home." She stood and stretched. "Where are you headed this morning?"

"I need to go back to the church." He hesitated, then added, "I would like the names of those who were killed yesterday so I can visit their families."

She frowned. "That sounds dangerous."

"It's not." He couldn't allow the two attempts on his life to prevent him from doing his duty. Maybe David and Goliath should be his theme for next Sunday. Bravery in the face of danger.

"I'll give you a ride."

"No need. It's only five blocks away." Her offer was nice, but he suspected she'd only made it because she thought Pinky might be at the church waiting for him.

"Humor me. After sitting outside all night, I'd feel better knowing you reached the church safely."

The stubborn tilt to her chin made him sigh. "Fine. Give me a few minutes and I'll be ready to go."

"Not a problem." She carried her empty mug to the kitchen counter and poured another half a cup of coffee. "No need to rush on my account."

Taking her at her word, he indulged in a quick shower, then donned what he thought of as his pastor uniform, black dress slacks and black shirt along with the white collar. He needed to be ready if victims' families decided to seek him out.

When he joined Raelyn, she was working her phone. "Any updates?"

"Not yet." She slipped the phone into her pocket. "Ready?"

"Yes." He led the way through the living room to the front door. He waited for her to step through, then locked the door behind him. When she headed for her squad, he hung back, struck by a sense of trepidation.

Maybe riding to church in a squad wasn't the smartest move.

"Something wrong?" Raelyn arched a brow. "What's the matter? You don't want any of your parishioners to see you hobnobbing with the police?"

"We're not hobnobbing." He squelched the urge to chuckle. "I'm more worried about your safety."

"We'll be fine." She waved off his concern. "Get in."

He opened the passenger-side door and slid in. He told himself it was foolish to worry. One thing about the neighborhood, things were generally quiet early in the morning. Those who worked the streets at night slept in.

"Are you planning to do more rideshare driving

tonight?" Raelyn asked as she pulled away from the curb, then drove around the block toward the New Hope Church.

"Depends." That was the other nice thing about being a rideshare driver. He could pick and choose his hours. "I want to be available at the church if anyone needs me."

That made her frown. "You need to be careful, Isaiah."

Her concern was heartwarming. The last person who'd warned him to be careful was his mother. And that was before he'd nearly died on the street.

"I will." The words no sooner left his mouth when there was a crack of gunfire followed by the shattering of the windshield.

"Down!" Raelyn hit the brake, then ducked her head. He could hear her giving their location to a dispatcher, requesting backup for an officer taking fire.

She was right about the danger. And this time, the shooter hadn't cared that he might kill Raelyn too.

CHAPTER FOUR

"Stay down, our backup is on the way." Raelyn didn't like staying inside the damaged squad, it felt as if they were sitting ducks in a pond surrounded by hunters. She poked her head up to scan the area for the shooter. She felt certain the large Black man who'd tried to choke Isaiah had done this.

Was this really because Isaiah had made an anonymous call to the police about a drug deal going down outside the church? It seemed a stretch. Although to be fair, she couldn't imagine why the kids had chosen that location in the first place.

Unless they'd assumed Isaiah wouldn't rat them out.

"Let me up," he said in a muffled voice.

"No. I'm wearing a vest. You're not." The vest wouldn't protect her head, and her tactical team helmet was in the trunk of the squad, far out of reach. She was surprised the shooter hadn't made another attempt, but then she heard the wail of sirens.

Reluctantly, she let Isaiah up. "The local cops are on the way."

He sat up, frowning at the damage to her squad. "I feel terrible that you were in harm's way. This is my fault."

She turned to look at him. "You do know who's behind this?"

"I don't." He grimaced. "I wish I did. I would gladly tell you."

Somehow, she didn't quite believe that. Yet he had made the anonymous call.

There had been three attempts on his life in less than twenty-four hours. And that meant Isaiah needed to be in a safe house.

She watched as the two squads came up to either side of her damaged police cruiser. She pushed out of the driver's side door and smiled when she saw Reed Carmichael. She knew Reed was married to Alanna Finnegan, her boss Rhy Finnegan's sister. "Hey, Reed. Glad to see you."

"Happy to be here considering I missed the action yesterday." He worked out of the fifth district, but those officers often backed up the third district. The way the maps were drawn, his precinct shared some of this same turf. His gaze was full of concern. "Is this a personal attack against you?"

"No." She glanced over to where Isaiah had gotten out of the squad and gestured to him. "Pastor Isaiah Washington. He's in charge of the New Hope Church."

Reed's eyebrow hiked up in surprise. "That's odd. Why would anyone target him?"

"He says he doesn't know." She thought about how Isaiah had once sold drugs on these streets. "This is the third attempt to kill him, though, so obviously something is going on."

Reed let out a low whistle. "That's not good. What about taking him into protective custody?"

"I was about to call Rhy to ask about that," she admitted.

"Will you please stop talking about me as if I'm not here?" Isaiah said testily. "Don't I have any say in this?"

She was tempted to say no but managed to hold back the retort. She drew a deep breath and turned to face him. "Let me guess. You want to go to the church as if this never happened."

He held her gaze, and she thought she caught a flash of regret. "That is what I'd like to do. But obviously I can't ignore what just happened here. I guess it's for the best if I return home and stay put for the next twenty-four hours."

"The large Black man who attacked you knows where you live," she felt compelled to point out. "Returning home is not a viable option."

"I don't have unlimited funds for a hotel." He frowned. "Although I could do a day or two, I guess."

"Let me give you both a ride out of here," Reed offered. He raked his gaze over her. "You look as if you could use some sleep."

That was putting it nicely. She knew she looked like leftover meatloaf. "I do; my shift is at three o'clock today." She hesitated, then added, "Let's go. I have an idea."

One of the other officers called for a tow truck for her squad. She tried not to think about what Rhy would say about the damaged car. He wouldn't blame her, but as the captain of their team, he had to deal with the never-ending budget issues.

A job she did not envy.

Once they were seated in Reed's squad, she turned in her seat to glance at Isaiah. "I have a second bedroom in my house. I think you should stay there for a while. I need to get some sleep before heading off to work my scheduled eight-hour shift. You'll have the place to yourself."

"Where is your house?" Isaiah asked.

"Greenland," she admitted. "I know that's about ten miles from your church, but it's the best I can do for tonight."

He turned to gaze out the window for a moment, then slowly nodded. "Okay. I'll stay with you temporarily."

"Thank you." She was surprised he agreed and felt as if a weight had rolled off her shoulders. Raelyn knew she wouldn't have gotten much sleep if he'd refused. Why she felt responsible for him, she had no idea. She pulled her phone from her pocket and called Rhy to fill him in on the latest.

"Are you hurt?" Rhy demanded.

"I'm fine and so is Pastor Washington." She sighed. "The squad took a hit, though. I'm with Reed Carmichael. He's dropping us at my place." She filled Rhy in on the choking attempt outside Isaiah's house.

"And Isaiah really has no idea who is behind all of this?" Her boss's tone reeked of doubt. She was glad she wasn't the only skeptic.

"That's what he says." She yawned as the adrenaline rush after being struck by gunfire faded. "I'm heading home to get some sleep."

"Do you want me to find someone to take your shift?" Rhy asked.

"No need." The last thing she wanted was to spend the entire day with Isaiah. Bad enough he'd be in her personal space. "I'll be fine."

"Keep in touch," Rhy said, before ending the call.

She slid her phone back into her pocket and yawned again. Her lack of sleep from sitting outside Isaiah's house was catching up with her.

Reed dropped her and Isaiah off in front of her small ranch house. "Call if you need anything, Rae."

"Will do. Thanks." She pulled her keys from her pocket and headed up to the front door. After unlocking it, she stepped inside, followed by Isaiah.

"This is very nice," he said with admiration.

"Probably not as welcoming as yours, though." She was keenly aware of the lack of personal items on display. Not that Isaiah had any family photos either. She thought about her mother and the way she'd been put into the foster care system after nearly being sexually assaulted and nearly raped by Kenny, her mother's boyfriend.

She hadn't seen her mother after that. And truthfully hadn't even tried to find the woman. The very fact that her mother had tried to defend her dirtbag boyfriend had hurt.

After living in various foster homes, then joining the army, she valued her privacy. She hadn't lived with anyone in years and was a little annoyed to have Isaiah invading her personal space now.

Yet she's the one who suggested this arrangement. She forced a smile. "Make yourself at home." She headed down the short hallway where the bedrooms were located. "Here's the guest room." She opened the door. "We have to share the full bathroom, but there's a half bath off the kitchen."

"The life of luxury," Isaiah murmured. His smile lit up his features, making her keenly aware of how handsome he was. "Thank you."

She nodded, suddenly at a loss for what to say. The house wasn't big or fancy, but it was hers. She made her way to the next doorway, leading into the main bedroom, then glanced at him over her shoulder. "Good night."

"Good night, Raelyn."

His deep husky voice seemed to follow her inside the

room. She closed the door and leaned against it for a long moment. Then she pushed away and removed her weapon, utility belt, and the rest of her gear.

Being in the army had trained her to sleep in difficult situations. But she soon learned that ignoring physical discomfort was far easier than ignoring her troubled thoughts and emotions.

As a result, sleep did not come easily.

ISAIAH WASN'T USED to sitting around doing nothing all day. He spent an hour or two working on his sermon for the upcoming Sunday, then decided to clean Raelyn's kitchen. He did the task as quietly as possible so as not to wake her.

He didn't used to be such a neat freak, but jail had changed him. He would never again take the simple things in life, like cleanliness, for granted.

Besides, he'd rather stay busy. He'd noticed Raelyn didn't have any family photos in the main living area. Or any other personal mementos. The same way he didn't. He'd often wished he had a picture of his mother. They had never owned a camera or those expensive cell phones that had cameras built in. It was only when he'd gotten out of jail and learned his mother had died that the realization had sunk deep.

All he had left of his mother was memories. And even those were fading with time.

He found himself wondering why Raelyn had chosen to live alone. Why she'd joined the army, then had become a cop. They were very different people, yet he couldn't help being intrigued by her.

When the kitchen was spotless, he tiptoed down the hall to listen at her door. Hearing nothing, he returned to the main living space.

Now what? He should have brought his Bible with him. Or another book to read. He had his cell phone and could use the reading app, which wasn't optimal but would do in a pinch.

He wasn't remotely interested in daytime TV.

Maybe this wasn't such a good idea. He would be far better off working as a rideshare driver rather than sitting around here. But he wouldn't leave without letting Raelyn know, so he forced himself to stay put.

Thinking she'd be hungry when she awoke, he poked through her fridge and freezer. He found ground beef and the rest of the ingredients he'd need to make a large pot of chili.

"Something smells great."

He whirled from the stove, his gaze colliding with Raelyn's. She was dressed casually in worn blue jeans and a light topaz long-sleeved T-shirt. It was the first time he'd seen her out of uniform, and his mouth went dry at how stunningly beautiful she was.

When he realized she was looking at him in amusement, he forced himself to turn his gaze back to the stove. "Chili," he managed in a choked voice that had nothing to do with the large Black man's attack on him the night before. "I hope you don't mind."

"I told you to make yourself at home." She crossed over to sniff at the pot. "Where did you learn to cook?"

"I taught myself." He smiled. "Prison food is awful."

"As bad as army rations, I'm sure." The way she returned his smile made his heart stutter in his chest. He put his hand up to press on the scar the bullet had left behind. "I would have made corn bread, but I couldn't find the ingredients for that."

"I've never made cornbread, although it sounds amazing." She finally moved away, going to the fridge to pour herself a glass of water. "Thanks for doing this. I only have forty minutes before I need to leave for work."

"I know. It's ready." He quickly filled two bowls and carried them to the table. Then he brought out the crackers he'd found in her cupboard. "I would like to say grace."

She nodded and bowed her head.

"Dear Lord Jesus, we thank You for this food we are about to eat. We ask that You continue to keep Raelyn and the other police officers safe in Your care. Amen."

There was a slight pause, before she added, "Amen."

They ate in silence for a moment. "I'd like to do some rideshare hours this evening," he said. "If I can't be at the church, supporting my parishioners, I'd at least like to do something constructive."

"I'm not sure that's a good idea," she said with a frown. "The large Black man who attacked you knows your car."

"Yes, that's true." He stared down at his bowl of chili, which was not bad if he said so himself. Then he lifted his gaze to hers. "I was thinking I could drop you off at work and borrow your vehicle. I noticed you have an SUV in the garage. I'll make sure to top off the gas tank. I'll have to log in to register the vehicle so I can use it, but that won't take long."

She looked as if she might refuse, then nodded. "Okay. I guess I can understand your desire to keep busy. I would go crazy sitting around too."

"Thanks." He smiled in relief. "I'm glad you understand."

She glanced around the kitchen. "I can't help but notice

you were so bored you cleaned." She shook her head. "That wasn't necessary."

"I don't mind." He shrugged and took another bite of his chili. "It's the least I can do while you put your life on the line for others."

"I appreciate that, but all you have to do is tell me who you think is coming after you," she said. "Maybe enemies from the past?"

"I'd considered that, but ten years is a long time." He paused, not sure how much to tell her. "Ten years ago, I only knew the name of the head of the drug-running operation as Chief. Which isn't much help."

"I can run the nickname through the system, see if anything hits," she mused. "You'd be surprised by the level of information the police have gathered over time."

He probably should have mentioned it earlier. "The other guy who worked the drug business is a Donte Wicks. Last I checked, he was still in prison. He's a tall skinny guy, so I don't believe he was the one who attacked me last night."

She gave him an exasperated look. "You should have told me about Donte Wicks. Could be the large Black man is a friend or family member of the guy."

"Maybe I should have, but the fact is there's always another drug dealer in the wings, ready to take over. I can't imagine someone trying to kill me just because Donte is in jail." He spread his hands. "Do you have any idea how many people who live where I do have done jail time? It's far more common to have a police record than not." He thought of Pinky and the Glock, and his heart felt heavy. "I can't imagine anyone would come after me ten years later for something like that. Especially when many of these guys are irrationally proud of serving time. For them, it's a badge of honor. Street cred."

"I guess that makes sense." She finished her chili. "This was delicious. Thanks."

"It's your food. I just threw it together." He rose to his feet and reached for her empty bowl. "I'll do the dishes while you finish getting ready for work."

"Isaiah." Hearing his name, he turned to glance back at her. "I want you to be cautious tonight, okay?"

"I will. There's no reason to worry; driving isn't very dangerous. Most of my customers ignore me."

She nodded, and he turned back to fill the sink with soapy water. Sure, there was always the possibility of being robbed while driving, but everyone knew that payments were made via electronic means rather than cash.

When the dishes were stacked in the sink, he left them to air dry. Raelyn returned to the kitchen, wearing a fresh uniform. With her hair pulled back in a bun, she wore what he thought of as her cop face. A serious expression that gave her an aura of authority.

"Ready?" She held out her keys.

"Yes." He opened the door leading to the garage. Minutes later, he was driving away from her ranch home toward the address she'd given him for the precinct.

"Do you go out on patrol?" He glanced at her, realizing he didn't know much about how the police operated. "Or wait for a specific type of call?"

"We do go out on patrol," she said. "But we're not given specific assignments like most cops because we may need to drop everything to head out on a specific tactical assignment." She frowned. "Much like the one we responded to yesterday outside your church."

"I see." It sounded as if she and her teammates

responded to the highest level of crime scenes, placing her and the others smack in the middle of danger. Granted, all cops were in danger; those who'd responded yesterday could attest to that. But still, he couldn't help being impressed with her dedication to service.

Maybe that dedication to serving the community was another way they were similar.

"I've never been inside a police station." He pulled up in front of the precinct. "I hope you have a safe and productive shift, Raelyn."

She nodded. "Thanks, you too." Without saying anything more, she slid out of the passenger seat and hurried up to the building. He shifted into drive and pulled away, reminding himself that despite their respective jobs of serving others, Raelyn was hardly the woman for him.

She was beautiful, smart, strong, and capable of protecting others. Even if she was looking for a relationship, she would not be interested in a man with a criminal record, who worked for peanuts as a pastor, and made ends meet by driving for a rideshare company. He preached peace and forgiveness, while she dressed each day for war with a gun on her hip and a bulletproof vest as a shield.

He needed to keep his head screwed on straight. The best he could do was to admire Raelyn from afar.

He pulled over to the side of the road to update the vehicle information in the rideshare app. Then he placed himself as available to provide rides. It didn't take long for the first request to come in, and he quickly accepted the job and turned around to head for the airport.

It had been a while since he'd made an airport run and found he liked it much better than late-night driving. However, he was usually at his church at this time of the day. That thought made him feel bad for the families that were grieving the loss of their loved ones without his support.

Was he being a coward to avoid returning to his job at the church? Yes, three attempts had been made against him, but what about the people who deserved his support? He couldn't hide at Raelyn's house forever.

Tomorrow, he decided. He'd return to his role as church pastor first thing in the morning. To be there for those who needed him.

The next couple of hours went by slowly. This sitting around, twiddling his thumbs, was the hardest part. At least the May weather was warm enough that he could sit in the park with the windows open.

His thoughts went back to the attack outside his house and the large Black man who'd told him he deserved to die. Had there been a hint of familiarity about him? Not Donte Wicks, but maybe someone close to Donte? A brother or cousin?

He abruptly straightened in the driver's seat. Was it possible that guy had been the Chief himself?

No, that wasn't likely. He relaxed, shaking his head at his own foolishness. Men who ruled the hood, the way the Chief did, wouldn't get their hands dirty by attacking him. He'd hire someone for that.

But even if the Chief was behind the attacks, he still didn't understand why. Isaiah's days of selling drugs were over and had been for ten years. He didn't know the guy's real name and doubted anyone else did either.

None of it made any sense. He sighed, then sat up straight when another call came in. He quickly accepted the job and started Raelyn's SUV.

Another ride, another dollar, he thought with a smile. At least he'd have some cash stockpiled for his after

Sunday service meals. And that alone was worth the effort.

He picked up another guy at the airport, then had a fare from a local hotel. He was about to call it a night when he was offered another job, picking up an older man from a nursing home to head to the hospital.

That was unusual enough that he accepted the ride and headed over. When the older man finally got settled in the back seat, he met his gaze in the rearview mirror. "Are you feeling okay, sir?"

"Fine, fine." He waved a gnarled hand. "Just gonna visit my wife, that's all."

"I understand." The news made him relax, and Isaiah decided to provide this ride for free. The older man gazed out the window, then turned to face him.

"Are you married?"

"Me? No." Raelyn's face flashed in his mind, and he ruthlessly shoved it away. "How long have you and your wife been married?"

"Fifty-eight years." A smile tugged at the corner of the man's mouth. "She's the light of my life."

Isaiah wondered what had caused her to be in the hospital but didn't ask. The trip was a short one, and when he pulled up in front of the main entrance, he said, "This ride is on me."

"Really?" The older man brightened. "Thank you. I appreciate that, and Lucy, my wife, will too."

Isaiah slid out from behind the wheel to help him out. "Take care of yourself."

"You too." The older man waved, then used his cane to head inside.

It was difficult to imagine being married to the same person for fifty-eight years. Marriages in the inner city did not last long. And many people didn't bother with the formality of getting married in the first place.

He slid back behind the wheel of Raelyn's SUV and turned to head back to her house. He'd done another four hours of driving, and that was good enough for now. Remembering his promise to fill her tank, he pulled into the gas station closest to her place. When he finished, he grabbed the receipt and then rounded the back of the vehicle to get inside.

Then he felt someone coming up behind him.

The recent attacks had him reacting with quick self-preservation instincts. He ducked and lashed out with his fist, striking the man's gun hand. He must have caught the guy off guard because the weapon clattered to the ground.

The large Black man, the same one who'd attacked him yesterday, threw a punch that he barely managed to deflect. When the assailant bent down to grab the gun he'd dropped, Isaiah brought his knee up into the man's face, striking him below the chin with as much strength as he could muster.

His attacker howled in pain and anger. Isaiah wanted this guy to be arrested and tossed in jail, but there wasn't a cop in sight.

"I'll kill you for this," the Black man hissed. As if that hadn't been his intent all along.

Isaiah didn't bother trying to reason with him. He knew he didn't have the other man's strength, so winning a fair fight wasn't going to happen. Feeling desperate, he lashed out with his foot, kicking the man in the groin. Once again, the assailant doubled over in pain but still managed to hang onto the gun.

Isaiah took advantage of the moment to jump into the SUV. He slammed and locked the doors, then drove off.

In the rearview mirror, he saw the large Black man lift the gun, pointing it toward him. He yanked hard on the steering wheel, taking the SUV up and over the curb to avoid being hit.

The Black man fired several rounds, but thankfully, none of them hit Raelyn's SUV.

He managed to drive away from the scene unscathed yet sick at the realization that the gunman had found him despite driving Raelyn's SUV.

And mere blocks from her ranch home.

He couldn't go back there, and neither could she. He made a fist and pounded on the steering wheel in frustration. His dark past had drawn Raelyn into danger right alongside him.

And he still had no idea who was behind this or why.

CHAPTER FIVE

When Raelyn's cell phone rang, she frowned at the number on the screen. Spam call? She was about to ignore it, but then changed her mind. Hesitantly, she answered, "Yeah?"

"This is Isaiah." His voice was tense but calm. "The same large Black man attacked me outside the gas station a few blocks from your house."

"How did he find you?" She glanced around the area she and Grayson had staked out. There had been no signs of activity, despite the lead they'd gotten about those kids from the church living in the neighborhood.

She was determined to find Pinky and the others. But especially Pinky. She was hoping to convince him to rat on the others.

"I don't know," Isaiah admitted. "But I don't dare go back to your house."

She caught Grayson's raised eyebrow at that comment but did her best to ignore it. "Okay, meet us back at the precinct. We'll come up with a plan B."

"Okay." There was a brief pause, then he added, "I'm

sorry, Raelyn. I never wanted to put you or anyone else in danger."

"It's fine." She appreciated his concern, but she was a trained cop. "See you in ten to fifteen."

"What's that about?" Grayson demanded as he put the squad in gear and pulled out of their parking spot.

She swallowed a sigh. "The preacher was attacked again. Head back to the precinct. It's clear this guy being in danger is related to whatever transpired outside the church yesterday."

"He's at your place?" Grayson asked incredulously. "What were you thinking?"

"I was thinking he'd be safe there." She grimaced. "It doesn't make sense that anyone from his neighborhood could have found him in Greenland."

"Are you sure he's being honest with you?" Grayson made a sharp U-turn to head back to the precinct. "You better talk to Rhy and Joe about this."

"I will." She had already spoken to Rhy, who hadn't been thrilled with her plan of having Isaiah stay with her, although he hadn't issued an order saying she couldn't move forward with the plan. Yet even so, he would not be happy to hear about this latest attempt against Isaiah.

Rhy and Joe were protective of their team. Her teammates were the only family she had, and she would have done anything to protect them too.

Her being in danger put those who worked with her at a higher risk. The situation made her angry, yet there wasn't anything she could do about it.

"I'm not waking Rhy up now," she said, belatedly realizing Grayson was looking at her expectantly. "He's likely sleeping, and I wouldn't want to risk waking Devon and Colleen." Rhy's daughter, Colleen, was only six months old.

From Raelyn's experience in the foster homes she'd stayed in, she knew that once you woke a baby, there was no sleeping the rest of the night.

"Tomorrow, first thing," Grayson said in agreement. "What's your plan for tonight?"

"We'll need to stay under the radar for a bit." She knew there were plenty of motels who would take cash from police officers with no questions asked. "I'd try the American Lodge, but I would hate for Gary to suffer more damage."

"We've taken care of his broken windows, so he doesn't hold it against us." Grayson shrugged. "And since Gary knows us, that's your best option."

"I guess." She didn't relish the idea of using connecting rooms in the American Lodge, partially because she didn't have a lot of cash on her. Her ranch house was small, but it had taken a big chunk of her savings, and she pretty much lived paycheck to paycheck these days.

The other reason she'd intended avoid the American Lodge was because it seemed like danger followed them there on a regular basis.

"Do you need money?" Grayson asked, reading her thoughts a little too well.

"I'm fine." She refused to take cash from her teammates. She'd use whatever was left in her checking from the closest ATM. Even though that would likely only last a day or two at the most.

It would have to be enough. She needed Isaiah to help her figure out what was going on. The fact that they hadn't found Pinky, or the other kids for that matter, nagged at her. Isaiah must know more about where they lived, where they chose to hang out when they weren't at his church services.

They needed answers and soon.

Grayson pulled up to the precinct. She was glad to see her SUV was already there with Isaiah behind the wheel. "Look, I need to get him settled, then I'll head back out to finish our stakeout."

"No need." Grayson waved her off. "Our shift ends at eleven thirty. Take the comp time." He flashed a grin. "I figure you deserve to get paid for grilling the preacher."

She hesitated, then nodded. No point in arguing. Besides, if Pinky and the others hadn't shown their faces by now, she had to assume they were tucked in for the night.

But where? That was the question.

"Thanks, Grayson." She slid out of the squad and jogged over to where Isaiah waited. He had the windows open, so she approached the driver's side door. "I need to head inside to change."

"Okay." His expression was troubled. "Although I would rather you remained armed in case that guy manages to find us again."

"Trust me, I'll have my weapon." She wasn't about to go anywhere without it. Not after everything that had transpired over the past twenty-four hours. "Stay put."

"I will."

She could feel his gaze boring into her back as she headed inside. Like most cops, she kept a change of clothes in her locker. Technically, they weren't supposed to wear their uniforms while off duty, but that rule wasn't always strictly enforced. But since she was off duty for the next two days, having worked the previous weekend, she absolutely needed to change.

She couldn't help feeling a bit naked without the uniform, vest, and utility belt as she joined Isaiah. Stepping up to the driver's side door, she gestured for him to come out.

He flashed a wry smile as he slid out. "I'm a good driver," he said as he stepped aside.

"Yeah, but it's my car." She didn't add that she was well trained in evasive techniques if they picked up a tail.

Once they were settled, she pulled away from the curb. Traffic was light this time of the night. She pulled up to the closest ATM.

"What are you doing?" Isaiah asked.

"We need cash for the motel." She pushed out of the driver's side door and quickly accessed the machine. She had twenty-five bucks in her pocket, which wouldn't get them very far.

"You should let me help pay for things," Isaiah said. "I'm the only reason you're in danger."

"Cops are always in danger." She took the cash and stuffed it into the front pocket of her jeans. "You can buy dinner. I'm starved."

"What would you like?" He seemed eager to pitch in, and his willingness to help reminded her of working with her teammates. But the preacher was far different from the cops she worked with. There wasn't an officer on the force who would hold back key information on an active investigation.

And she had a feeling Isaiah hadn't told her everything he knew.

"Raelyn?"

His deep voice interrupted her troubled thoughts. She tried to think of something that would fill her belly without costing a lot. "A sub sandwich. But we'll have to hurry to get there before they close."

"Sounds good." He pulled cash from his pocket, ready to pay for their meals.

Getting the sandwiches and two bottles of water didn't

take long. When she pulled into the parking lot of the American Lodge, Isaiah looked at the white two-story building with frank curiosity. "You know the owner?"

"Yeah." She threw the gearshift into park. "Gary is a former firefighter injured in the line of duty. He opened this place and gives special rates to cops and firefighters." She grimaced. "We've used his place a lot over the past year and a half. One added benefit is that he has several security cameras." She didn't point out that the security cameras had not prevented several shoot-outs from taking place at the motel. Poor Gary had been forced to replace several windows and repair drywall that had been damaged by bullets. The team had paid for the repairs.

But not tonight. She had not seen anyone behind them during the entire ride out to Brookland. She was confident they were safe here.

"Looks nice," Isaiah said, joining her.

A familiar clerk was at the front desk. "Hey, James. It's been a while."

"Officer Lewis," James responded with a nod. He looked curiously at Isaiah who still wore his black shirt and slacks. "I take it you need a couple of rooms?"

"Connecting rooms, yes, please." She dug for her cash. "Let Gary know we appreciate his support."

"Will do." James took the cash and handed over two room keys. "You can have the connecting rooms at the top of the stairs."

"Thanks." She knew exactly where they were, as Joe and Elly had used the same set of rooms in the past. She led the way outside and took the stairs to the second level. She'd purposefully parked in the center of the motel, away from the two sets of connecting rooms.

The more anonymity, the better.

"Open your side, okay?" She didn't wait for an answer but handed Isaiah a key to his room, then entered hers. These two rooms had been renovated last January and still held the faint scent of fresh paint.

Isaiah opened his connecting door at the same time she opened hers. She crossed the threshold, eyeing the sandwiches and water he'd set on the small table of his room.

She decided to wait until after they'd eaten to question him. Dropping into the closest chair, she kept her hands in her lap, knowing he'd want to say grace.

"Dear Lord Jesus, we are grateful for the protection You have provided for us. We humbly ask that You continue to keep us safe in Your care. Amen."

"Amen." It seemed impolite not to respond in kind. She unwrapped her sub and dug in. "Thanks for dinner."

"This is the least I can do." His dark eyes were troubled. "I hate knowing I placed you in danger."

"You must have gotten a better look at the man who attacked you tonight." She held his gaze.

"I did." He looked thoughtful for a moment. "I didn't recognize him, though."

She scowled. "You really expect me to believe that?"

His eyes darkened with anger. "Yes, I do. I am not protecting him, why should I? But you must know that he's not the type to attend my services. And as much as I try to mingle with the neighbors, it's not as if I'm automatically welcomed with open arms. There's a lot of distrust, despite the support I've gotten from the mayor."

She supposed that much was true. "Are you absolutely sure he's not a drug dealer like Donte Wicks?"

"No, I'm not at all certain of that. He very well could be." He set his sandwich down and reached for his water. "I wondered if the large Black man was the guy in charge, but then doubted he'd come after me himself."

She hated to admit his logic made sense. She abruptly straightened. "Your phone."

"What about it?" He looked confused.

"That's what you use to do your rideshare work, right?" She mentally kicked herself for being so stupid. "Shut it down, now. We'll need to get rid of it."

"I already powered it down," he admitted, pulling it from his pocket and showing her the blank screen. "Although I have no idea how anyone could have tracked my phone."

She sagged into her chair with a sigh of relief that he'd been smart enough to shut the thing off. "We'll pick up a replacement disposable phone in the morning. Does the church pay for the phone and your plan?"

"No, I do." He shrugged, leaving the phone sitting on the table between them. "The mayor offered to foot the bill, but since I do the rideshare thing on the side, I decided it was better if I paid for it myself. I can deduct it as an expense."

"Okay, so maybe someone has the skills to figure out you're a rideshare driver and was able to track you that way." She wasn't sure how that was possible. She'd have to ask their tech support expert, Gabe Melrose, about that tomorrow. "That means we're safe here tonight."

"I'm glad." He looked relieved, and she realized she'd been pretty hard on him. Maybe he was being honest with her. Maybe he truly didn't understand why he'd been targeted.

The problem was that if Isaiah didn't have any information to offer, they were right back to square one. Without a single lead to follow.

And that did not bode well for her ability to get to the bottom of this mess.

ISAIAH KNEW he shouldn't be hurt that Raelyn didn't have much faith in him. To be honest, if the situation were reversed, he'd have trouble believing him too.

"Raelyn, I would never willingly put you or anyone else in harm's way." He searched her tawny gaze. "Never."

She flushed and looked away. "I hear you, but the fact is that without an ID on this guy, we've got nothing."

There was a long moment of silence. He felt bad about the situation too.

"I know." She abruptly smiled. "I'll have you go through mug shots. The odds are in our favor that your assailant has a criminal record." Her amber eyes gleamed with anticipation. "I'd head there tonight, but it will take time to get the computer system to spit out suspects that fit the general description you have already provided, and I'll need Gabe's help with that. But for sure, we'll head back to the precinct to work on that first thing in the morning."

"I'm happy to do that," he agreed. His mission in life was to save the children, but the large Black man had already chosen his path of crime. "I'm sure you're right about him being in the system."

"I'd be shocked if he wasn't," she said with satisfaction. "I'm glad we have a plan moving forward."

"Me too." He wondered if she'd looked at his mug shot while she'd been out on patrol. It would be in the same computer system. For some reason, the idea bothered him, and he told himself not to be foolish. His past had made him the man he was today.

He couldn't regret being given a second chance. This was God's plan. He could only hope he was up to the task God had set before him.

"You know, I don't really think my home has been compromised," she said thoughtfully. "If the perp was tracking your phone, he wouldn't necessarily know where I live."

"Maybe not." He shrugged. "But I wasn't willing to take that risk."

She looked as if she wanted to say more but popped the last bite of her sub sandwich into her mouth. Then she gathered her garbage together and drank what was left in her bottle of water. "Thanks. That hit the spot."

"Of course." He didn't want their time together to end, but of course, she needed sleep. And so did he. "Good night, Raelyn."

"Good night." She rose and moved across the room, pausing at the open doorway between their rooms. "I would like you to keep your side of the connecting door unlocked, just in case. And I'll do the same."

"That's not a problem." He would never infringe on her privacy. "Thanks for everything."

She nodded, then crossed the threshold.

Isaiah washed up in the small bathroom, then slid out of his black dress slacks and shirt. He crawled into bed wearing his T-shirt and boxers. He told himself not to think about Raelyn sleeping on the other side of the wall.

He was a man, not a monk. And he hadn't spent this much time in close proximity with an attractive woman in what seemed like forever. His one and only girlfriend, Shondra, had left him for Beau Critten, the mayor's son during their senior year of high school. He hadn't dated anyone seriously in the ten years since.

But Raelyn was different. She made him wish for something he couldn't have. No way would he cross the line, though, so he would do his best to ignore the weird awareness that seemed to shimmer between them. Especially since she had not given any indication that she felt the same way.

The cop and the preacher, he thought with a wry smile. *As if that would ever work.*

He must have dozed because he abruptly awoke, his heart hammering in his chest. He'd been dreaming of the gunfire, only this time, the shooter had been aiming at Raelyn instead of at him.

For a moment, he forgot where they were, then remembered the American Lodge motel. He swung up into a sitting position, straining to listen.

Muted voices wafted toward him. The television? Or was Raelyn talking to someone?

He stood and quickly pulled his clothes on. Upon moving toward the connecting door, he could hear the voices louder now.

Not the television, but Raelyn.

"We'll be there shortly," she said. A brief pause, then, "Because I want to see the damage for myself."

Damage? He sucked in a harsh breath. Her house?

He pushed her connecting door open and stepped inside. She was dressed, her expression somber.

"See you soon." She slid the phone into her pocket and looked at him. "I didn't mean to wake you, but I'm glad you're up."

"What happened?"

"That was Grayson. Someone torched my house." She looked angry rather than upset, although he imagined she was both. She grabbed her weapon and keys from the nearby table. "Let's go."

He wasn't about to argue. "Give me a sec to grab my shoes."

Two minutes later, they were headed down the stairs to the parking lot. He noticed that Raelyn scanned the area carefully as they made their way toward her SUV. He remembered her comment about there being security cameras and wondered who watched them overnight.

Probably no one, he thought grimly. He slid into the passenger seat as she took the wheel.

"How did Grayson hear about your house?" he asked.

"Colin Finnegan is a firefighter, and he was called to the scene. He must have recognized the address and tried to call me, but I was asleep. Somehow, he got in touch with Grayson."

"Oh, are you and Grayson seeing each other?" The thought was depressing.

"What? No!" She shot him an exasperated look. "I would never date one of the guys on the team. I'm sure he called Rhy who let him know Grayson and I were on the evening shift."

"Oh, I see." She tossed the names around as if they should mean something to him, only they didn't. "Rhy is your boss, right?"

"Right." She scowled. "I guess I was wrong about my place not being compromised. I'm sure the guy who attacked you is behind this."

"Yeah." He hated to admit she was probably right. Yet the idea that his assailant would take out his frustration on Raelyn filled him with anger. He was the one the Black guy wanted. Then a horrible thought hit.

"The church." He reached over to grasp Raelyn's arm,

keeping his voice even with an effort. "I think it's entirely possible this guy will target the New Hope Church next."

"I'll call it in." She used the hands-free function of the SUV to make the call. He listened as she spoke to the dispatcher on duty. "This is Officer Lewis. Someone has started my home on fire, and I need you to alert the third district to head straight over to the New Hope Church to make sure that building hasn't been hit too."

"Roger that, Officer Lewis," the dispatcher responded. "Contacting the third district now. I'll keep you updated."

"Thanks. End call." The screen went dark. She glanced at him. "I'm sorry. I hope the church hasn't been damaged too."

He could only nod in agreement. In truth, the church should have been the first target, not her home. But he had a bad feeling the assailant knew he'd be more upset at the damage to Raelyn's home. It was her personal space and shouldn't have factored into the assailant's plan.

Sure, he cared about the church, too, but that was a public meeting place. Technically, he could hold his services anywhere, had even held them in the local school's gymnasium when vandals had struck the church last year.

But her home? He hated that she'd suffer because of him.

Why, Lord, why?

God did not provide an answer.

Not that he'd really expected one. Except for the night he'd died and nearly went to heaven, God had not spoken directly to him in words.

But he often felt the Lord's guidance as he provided sermons for the congregation.

"Oh no," Raelyn whispered. He reached for her hand

when he saw the flicker of flames coming from her living room window.

To his surprise, she gripped his hand hard. She slowed to a stop at the end of the road where a large fire truck blocked their way.

"It's going to be a total loss," she said in a flat, dull voice.

He swallowed hard, silently agreeing with her. Then she pulled out of his grasp and shot out of the car.

"Wait!" He scrambled to catch up. She pushed past the fire truck, then stood with her mouth agape as several fire-fighters battled the blaze.

She was right. The place was too far gone to save.

A man jogged over to them. "Rae, you shouldn't have come. There's nothing you can do."

She didn't answer, her gaze seemingly fixed on the fire. The homes weren't too far away from each other, and he hoped the blaze wouldn't move from her ranch house to the neighbors on either side.

"You must be the preacher." The man standing beside Raelyn held out his hand. "Grayson Clark. I work with Raelyn."

He vaguely recognized the guy from the day of the shooting. It was difficult to comprehend how a fatal shoot-out in the north side of the city had caused this cascade of events leading to a raging fire burning Raelyn's home.

His fault. He'd made the phone call that had started the entire thing.

"There's nothing you can do," Grayson repeated. "Colin told me they're asking Mitch Callahan to investigate since we all know this was likely arson."

She nodded. "That's good."

Grayson stood there for a few more minutes, then

glanced at his watch. "I have to work tomorrow, so I need to hit the road. You should head back to the motel too."

She nodded without responding, her gaze still locked on the fire. The crew had battled it back, but the smoke was still thick in the air.

Grayson glanced at him, shrugged, and turned away. Isaiah moved closer to Raelyn, putting his arm around her shoulders. "I'm so sorry."

"It's not your fault." Her voice cracked, and he realized with horror that this strong woman was on the verge of tears.

Then she turned into his arms, burying her face against his chest. He wrapped his arms around her, holding her close and wishing more than anything there was a way to fix this.

But all he could do was pray.

CHAPTER SIX

Raelyn leaned gratefully against Isaiah's chest, unable to keep her emotions in check. The house was just a brick-and-mortar building. Life was more precious than anything else. Yet the small ranch home represented her independence, her rise above the streets of Chicago's South Side.

And now it was gone.

When Isaiah gathered her close, she reveled in his embrace. It had been a long time since she'd been held by a man. At least two years.

Men generally disappointed her. Her last boyfriend had cheated on her because she had refused to jump into bed with him. She knew she was better off without Rob. But that didn't mean she was ready to trust again.

"We should get out of here, Raelyn," Isaiah whispered.

She nodded against him but didn't move away. Oddly, she was content in his arms. Maybe she didn't entirely trust that he was telling her the truth, but she knew one thing for certain: Isaiah would never hurt her.

After a long moment, she gathered her strength and determination to pull away, subtly swiping at her damp eyes. "Thanks." She avoided his gaze in the darkness. "I rarely fall apart like this."

"You didn't fall apart at all," Isaiah murmured. He reached up and tucked a strand of her hair behind her ears, sending a tingle of awareness down her spine. "You're the strongest woman I know."

She managed to pull herself together. This wasn't the time to be hyperaware of Isaiah as an attractive man. It wasn't as if she would ever be interested in dating a preacher. As soon as the thought formed, she had to amend it. Isaiah wasn't just a pastor, he had grown up on the streets of the city.

The same way she had. Ironically, they had that in common.

Maybe she and Isaiah were more alike than she cared to admit.

"We'd better head back to the American Lodge." She glanced back at her house, relieved to see the fire was mostly out. She'd have to call her insurance company. With a sudden jolt, she realized the only items she owned were the clothes she was wearing. And her car.

Fresh tears threatened, but she told herself there was no point in thinking about what she'd lost. Things. Possessions that could be easily, if costly, to replace. It wasn't as if she had personal items inside.

She hadn't wanted any photographs of her mother. The woman who'd refused to believe Kenny had tried to rape a thirteen-year-old kid.

No, she was better off on her own. Now and always.

"Raelyn . . ." He sighed as his voice trailed off. "I wish there was something I could do for you."

She squared her shoulders and nodded. "You can help

by going through the mug shots tomorrow to find the man who attacked you. He must be involved in this."

"Of course." He rested his hand on her arm. "Come with me now. I'll drive us back to the motel."

"I can drive." She regretted her moment of weakness. "I'll be fine. Everything inside the house can be replaced."

He nodded in understanding and dropped his hand. She instantly missed the warmth of his fingers. Grayson was right, she shouldn't have come. All she'd done was fall apart during a time she needed to be on full alert. To find the assailant who had tried to kill Isaiah and now had also struck out at her personally.

With her back straight with steely determination, she slid in behind the wheel of her SUV. Isaiah didn't say anything, but his intense blue eyes glanced at her often. She did her best to ignore him.

The ride back to Brookland didn't take long, as it was half past three in the morning. She doubted she'd get any more sleep but knew they both needed to get more rest.

Come dawn, they'd have a long day ahead of them.

"What time would you like to head to the precinct?" Isaiah asked as they took the stairs up to their rooms.

She was going to suggest seven but then remembered Gabe didn't come in until eight. "Eight o'clock. We can grab something for breakfast on the way. Oh, and we'll need that replacement phone for you as well."

"I'll be ready." He flashed a lopsided smile. "Good night, Raelyn."

"Good night." She stepped back and closed the connecting door between their rooms. Not all the way, but enough to offer privacy.

The army had taught her to sleep under difficult

circumstances, but the image of the flames engulfing her home were seared into her mind.

She'd set her phone alarm for seven a.m., and when the device chirped, she bolted upright, stunned to realize she had fallen asleep. Still, she felt groggy when she silenced the alarm and headed into the bathroom.

The motel rooms had small coffeemakers, and she gratefully brewed a cup. She'd need caffeine to help get her through the next several hours. As she sipped her coffee, she heard movement from Isaiah's room. Rising from the edge of the bed, she opened her side of the connecting door. His side was wide open, so she poked her head in.

"You're ready?" He was dressed and sipping coffee, too, although the shadow of stubble on his cheeks belied a restful night.

"Yes." He smiled. "I heard your alarm."

"Sorry about that." She should have considered the sound would wake him.

"Don't be. I'm anxious to be of service." He took another sip of his coffee. "We have time for a real breakfast. My treat."

He'd paid for their subs last night, too, and she appreciated his willingness to cover their meals. Especially now when she had no idea what her homeowner's deductible would cost. Who paid attention to that kind of thing? "Okay, let's hit the road."

He drained his cup and set it aside. She did the same, then headed out of the room and down the stairs. Scanning the area, she saw nothing threatening.

Yet after the attack on Isaiah and the fire, she knew they needed to get a clean vehicle. One that couldn't be traced to either of them.

After breakfast, she told herself. She'd work on that, along with getting a replacement phone and notifying her insurance company while Isaiah was going through mug shots.

"Any place in particular you'd like to eat?" She glanced at Isaiah.

"I'm afraid I don't know this area. Whatever you suggest is fine."

She nodded. "There's a great place called Rosie's Diner. Rosie is Irish and always has fresh baked goods to go along with her huge breakfast menu."

"That sounds great."

She'd learned about the place from the Finnegan family. Colin in particular was a fan favorite. She sobered, remembering how Colin Finnegan had fought the fire at her ranch house last night.

The diner wasn't too far from the precinct, and despite the early hour, the place was busy. Rosie was building a reputation, and if her business kept booming like this, she'd have to find a larger building.

She and Isaiah had to wait a few minutes for a booth to open. Rosie quickly cleared the dishes, then waved them over. The older woman's eyes brightened when she recognized her.

"Ach, Raelyn, nice to see you again, lass!" Rosie beamed at Isaiah. "And you've brought a guest. Who is this fine young lad?"

"Rosie, this is Pastor Isaiah Washington. Isaiah, the infamous Rosie."

"A pleasure to meet you." He sniffed the air appreciatively. "Is that an apple turnover I smell?"

"Good nose," Rosie said with a heartly laugh. "I'll be bringing you a sample soon. Coffee?"

"Yes, please." She and Isaiah took their seats across from each other as Rosie bustled off. "Isn't she amazing?"

"This is a great place," he agreed. "I haven't had home-baked goods in—forever."

"I hear you on that." She sat back, pleased that he liked the place. Then she wondered why it mattered. This was a temporary arrangement. It wasn't like their worlds would ever meet except in times of violence.

And wasn't that a sad thought? Yet this was the world they lived in, so she did her best to brush it off.

"I'd like to say grace," Isaiah murmured, after they had steaming coffee and fresh apple turnovers.

She was accustomed to this by now, so she rested her hands in her lap and bowed her head.

"Lord Jesus, we thank You for this food and for keeping us safe in Your care. We ask that You continue to provide guidance and strength as we seek those who wish us harm. Amen."

"Amen." Surprisingly, his words resonated within. She did feel stronger today and just as determined to find the man responsible. And for the first time, it occurred to her that she should thank God that she and Isaiah weren't sleeping in her ranch house last night. The way the big Black man may have assumed.

Isaiah took a bite of his apple turnover and nearly groaned. "This is the best ever!"

She sampled hers too. "Delicious."

By the time they'd finished their baked goods, their breakfasts arrived. Isaiah had ordered the full Irish, while she'd settled for a veggie omelet.

"This is worth every penny," Isaiah declared when they were finished. "I wish I lived closer so I could eat here more often."

"I have to be careful not to eat here on a regular basis, or I'd never fit into my uniform," she joked.

"Ach, lass, is there anything more I can get for you?" Rosie cleared their dirty dishes.

"Just the check, please." Isaiah grinned. "Thank you for the best breakfast I've ever had, Rosie."

"Ach, you're a sweet talker, aren't ya?" Rosie laughed. "I like that."

Isaiah left money on the table, then they both rose to their feet. They didn't linger as there was a line forming at the door.

"That was wonderful, Raelyn. Thanks." Isaiah settled in the passenger seat. "A very nice way to start what I'm sure will be a difficult day."

"Yes." She knew what he meant. It was important to take time to enjoy the smaller things in life. "It's too early to get a phone, so we'll head to the precinct. We need to find the man who attacked you."

"I pray I do."

They rode in silence to the precinct. She parked her SUV in the back. There were two undercover vehicles parked back there too. And she hoped Rhy would allow her to use one of them for the next day or so.

As they headed inside, the irony of the situation washed over her. It wasn't that long ago that Steele and Brock had been in tight spots, similar to what she faced now.

She could only hope that this investigation would come to a positive resolution the way theirs had.

She lifted her gaze to the blue, cloud-dotted sky. And maybe she and Isaiah would need God's help to make that happen.

THE POLICE PRECINCT was busy this morning. A few of the officers eyed Isaiah curiously, but most ignored him, intent on their respective tasks. Isaiah had to admit that it was interesting to see this side of law enforcement. Men and women doing their best to keep the community safe.

Like Raelyn and those she worked with. Of course, the neighborhood he lived in didn't have a positive attitude toward the police. And he was ashamed to admit that he'd once felt the exact same way.

It wasn't an issue of race, although that sometimes played a role. There were plenty of Black and Hispanic officers too. No, the real issue was poverty, lack of education, and gun violence.

Without money, the residents on the north side couldn't buy cars or afford to travel for work. He knew, better than most, the lure of easy money outweighed legit employment at minimum wage.

He stifled a sigh, knowing that he could only do so much. And today that meant finding the large Black man who'd attacked him.

Who'd attempted to kill him.

"Have a seat." Raelyn gestured to an empty desk. "I'll get Gabe started on the search parameters."

"Okay." He lowered himself into a chair, prepared to wait. The more he thought about it, the more convinced he was that this must be related to the drug dealing he'd done in the past. Maybe the large Black man was related to Donte Wicks. Ten years was a long time to hold a grudge, but that was the only angle he could come up with.

"Well, if it isn't the preacher." The dry tone had him glancing up in surprise. He recognized Raelyn's fellow cop Grayson. There was a hint of anger in the man's eyes.

"Have you finally decided to cooperate with the investigation?"

"I've been cooperating all along," he said in protest. "I told Raelyn everything I know."

Grayson's dark eyes were skeptical. "Sure you have."

He couldn't sway this man's opinion of him, so he changed the subject. "When will you know how the fire started at Raelyn's house?"

Grayson's brown gaze turned serious. "Fire Investigator Mitch Callahan is heading there now. It may be too hot to learn much, but he'll start poking around for answers."

"I pray he can find something useful."

"Oh hey, Grayson." Raelyn strode toward them, a laptop computer in hand. "What are you doing here so early?"

"Checking in on you and the case." Grayson gestured to the computer. "What's that for?"

"Isaiah is going to search mug shots for the man who assaulted him." She set the computer on the desk, opened the lid, and logged on. "Here you go." She turned the device toward him. "I need to chat with Rhy. Let someone know if you find him."

"I will." He turned his attention to the laptop. There was no reason to be jealous of Grayson. Raelyn said they were teammates, nothing more. Yet he couldn't help noticing that Grayson fit into her life far better than he ever could.

It didn't matter. He used the track pad to begin scrolling through the mug shots. He took his time, examining each face closely before moving on to the next. He didn't want to make a mistake.

Not with something this important.

Besides, he wouldn't be able to live with himself if he identified the wrong man.

He'd scrolled through a dozen images when Raelyn returned. To his surprise, she set a disposable phone on the desk beside him. "I asked Grayson to pick this up for you. How is it going? I'd offer you coffee, but the stuff they brew here is like sludge."

"That's okay. I've had enough." He pocketed the phone and turned back to the screen. "It's going well, but I haven't found him yet."

"Rhy had given us permission to use the undercover Jeep." She shrugged. "That should help us fly under the radar."

"That's good." He glanced back at her. "And your insurance company?"

She wrinkled her nose. "Calling them next. Let me know if you find him."

"I will." He watched as she moved to another empty desk to make the call, then went back to work. He'd gone through another five mug shots and was beginning to fear his guy wasn't in the system at all, when he found him.

He sat back in the chair, his gaze focused on the man's unsmiling face. He knew with absolute certainty this was the man who'd attacked him.

Hugo Morrison. Not Donte Wicks, but there was still the faint resemblance to Donte's features. Maybe a half brother or cousin. He glanced over to where Raelyn was still on the phone. She had her forehead propped in one hand as she spoke, making him think the news wasn't good.

Well, knowing the identity of the man who'd done this would make her feel a little better. He turned back to the computer, not surprised to see that Hugo had done time for carjacking and armed robbery.

What had caused Hugo to escalate to attempted murder? Had the Chief put him up to it? Was this related to the drug deal that had gone down outside his church or from his actions ten years ago?

They wouldn't get answers until they had Hugo in custody. Hopefully sooner rather than later.

Raelyn stood and came over to join him. Her expression was strained, but she simply gestured to the computer. "You found something?"

"Yes. This is the guy. Hugo Morrison." He turned the screen so she could see it better. "I'm positive he's the one behind this."

Her expression brightened. "Good job, Isaiah. We'll issue a BOLO for him ASAP. And we'll send a unit to his last-known address too."

"Happy to help." He wondered if their time together would end once they had Hugo in custody.

"Sit tight." She grabbed the computer and headed toward one of the nearby offices. "Rhy? We have him!"

Ridiculous to be disappointed at the news the danger was likely over. It was better this way—he needed to get back to his church duties, and Raelyn needed to focus on her own situation. He hoped her insurance would put her up somewhere while the ranch house was being repaired.

And how long would that take? Weeks? Months? A year? He grimaced, suspecting the worst-case scenario.

"Pastor Washington?" A tall blond man strode toward him. His name tag identified his last name as Finnegan. He remembered meeting Rhy Finnegan the day of the shooting. "I understand you've identified our perp."

"Yes." He rose to his feet. "Please, call me Isaiah. I hope the officers on the street will find him very soon."

"We will." Rhy smiled grimly. "We appreciate your

help on this."

"Of course." He glanced over to where Raelyn was once again talking on the phone. "I have a question, though. Have you heard if my church is still okay?"

"Yes, my brother-in-law Reed Carmichael sat outside the place last night," Rhy said. "I know it's not technically in his district, but he volunteered. I admire what you're trying to do there."

"Trying is the key word," he said lightly. "It's often an uphill battle."

"I can imagine." Rhy's expression was somber. "I understand you were also the one who anonymously called the police about the drug deal going down outside the church."

"Yes." He still felt guilty over that. "I gave Raelyn—er, Officer Lewis the street names of the kids who came through the church. I don't know their legal names."

"I understand. We've put those names and the nickname 'Chief' through the system but haven't gotten any hits." Rhy frowned. "You're sure there isn't anything else you can tell us?"

"Ten years ago, I worked for Donte Wicks, who supposedly took orders from the Chief. I checked just a few weeks ago, and Donte was still in jail. The kid who shot me so he could steal the drugs, was Petey Dobbs. I gave his name to the officers after I recovered from surgery, and they told me they found him dead of a drug overdose." Justice at its best, he'd thought at the time. "I don't remember giving them Donte Wick's name, but I was in and out during much of those early days. There were likely other drug runners, but Hugo wasn't involved back then as far as I know."

"Maybe we can arrange to visit Donte Wicks in jail," Rhy said thoughtfully. "I doubt he'll cooperate with us, but it's worth a try."

"Don't get your hopes up," he warned. "Doing jail time is a badge of honor to some of these guys. If Donte hasn't given up the Chief by now, I doubt he'll suddenly change his mind."

"Maybe not, but it's a stone that needs to be overturned just in case." Rhy clapped him on the back. "Thanks again. Take care of yourself. My family and I will keep you and your parish in our prayers."

"Thanks, you too." He was a little surprised by the easy acceptance from the captain of the tactical team.

"Isaiah?" Raelyn rushed over, and he wondered when she'd changed into her uniform. His no-nonsense cop was back. He preferred her softer side. "We have a lead on Pinky."

His gut clenched. Of all the kids who had attended his church services and the meal afterward, he'd sincerely hoped Pinky would find his way out of the life of crime. He cared about that boy, maybe because he saw himself in the kid's features. Especially in the young boy's tortured eyes. If God had chosen to save Isaiah, surely He could do the same for Pinky.

"Did you hear me?" She looked exasperated. "Let's go. I want you to come with me."

That made him frown. "Why? I'm not a cop."

"Pinky held you at gunpoint, remember?" She searched his gaze for a long moment. "We need that gun. Even if Pinky didn't fire it, we need to know if that weapon was used to kill a cop and seriously injure two others."

He didn't want to go but didn't see another option. Maybe he could convince Pinky to tell the truth about what happened outside the church.

Would Raelyn or other cops even bother to listen?

"Okay." He forced himself to nod in agreement. "I'll come with you."

"Good. We'll take the Jeep." She led the way through the precinct to the door leading to the rear parking lot. He followed, wrestling with his feelings. He wanted to protect Pinky.

Yet maybe Pinky needed to do his part. The way he had.

He didn't say anything as Raelyn drove them to the north side of Milwaukee. The familiar dilapidated homes bothered him more for some reason, maybe because he'd spent the last twenty-four hours away from the obvious signs of poverty and despair.

The American Lodge motel was nothing fancy, but he knew most if not all the residents here would switch places in a heartbeat.

"Where are we going?" he asked, breaking the prolonged silence.

Raelyn rattled off the address. "Do you know it?"

"No." He wondered where they'd learned that information, then decided it didn't matter.

Raelyn pulled up in front of the house, eyeing the structure warily. It was in rough shape, like most of the homes around here. Then she pushed out of the Jeep.

He did the same, walking beside her as they mounted the rickety steps to the front door.

She knocked, and of course, no one answered. She pounded again, harder. After a long moment, an older Black woman swung the door open. "What?" Her voice was not friendly.

"I need to speak with Pinky," Raelyn said.

The woman crossed her arms over her chest. "Pinky don't live here."

"Please," he urged, speaking up. "We simply want to talk to him, that's all."

The woman snorted, then stepped back. "You want to check for yourself, Preacher? Go ahead."

Raelyn frowned, then entered the home. He stayed close but already knew they wouldn't find Pinky. This woman wouldn't have let them in if the kid had been there.

The search didn't take long. Raelyn pasted a smile on her face. "Thanks for your cooperation."

The woman scowled without saying a word. She did slam the door shut behind them, though, making her displeasure known.

"That was a bust," Raelyn said.

"Maybe Pinky was there but took off." He shrugged. "These kids stay on the move to avoid getting caught."

"Yeah, I guess." She looked determined now. "We'll have another officer stake the place out to see if Pinky returns tonight."

"I'd like to head to the church for a few minutes. I keep a spare set of clothes there."

"Fine." She slid in behind the wheel, giving the woman's house one last look before driving away.

Thankfully, New Hope Church looked exactly the way he'd left it. No additional graffiti and no sign of a forced entry. He unlocked the door and stepped inside, scanning the room. Then he narrowed his gaze when he saw something dark sitting in the middle of the white tablecloth on the altar.

He rushed forward, hardly able to believe his eyes. Raelyn came up next to him. "Is that the Glock?"

"I don't know." Despite saying the words, he was sure it was.

And he was convinced Pinky had left it there.

CHAPTER SEVEN

Thankfully, Raelyn's uniform utility belt contained a few evidence bags. First, she took several pictures with her cell phone, showing the weapon sitting on the white tablecloth. She carefully used one as a glove to place the weapon inside, then sealed it shut. One Glock looked just like another, but she could tell by the resigned expression in Isaiah's blue eyes that he suspected this was the weapon Pinky had held pressed against his side that day.

She did too. Especially since the gun was left in the church as a silent message to Isaiah. Almost like an apology for holding him at gunpoint.

"We'll head back to the precinct so I can get this processed." The lab had the bullets that were removed from the dead officer and the two who were critically injured. One of the wounded officers, a guy named Brett Carson, was doing better, awake but still on pain meds. The other was still listed in critical condition. According to her brief conversation with Rhy, they were hoping to be able to interview Carson about what had happened soon.

She would bet her next paycheck that this Glock had

fired the rounds that had hit at least one of those officers, if not all three. She found herself hoping that Carson would be able to identify the kid who shot him, and that Pinky wasn't responsible.

Maybe she was getting soft or was swayed by Isaiah's view on things, but she found it hard to imagine Pinky as a cold-blooded killer.

"I need to check the back." Isaiah turned and hurried down to his office. She followed more slowly, resting one hand on the butt of her gun in case Pinky or someone else was back there and still armed.

She relaxed when she realized the office and small kitchen area were empty. Then she frowned. "The front door of the church was locked. How did Pinky get in?"

"You don't know who left that gun there," he said mildly. "But how someone got inside is exactly what I'm trying to determine."

She followed him through the small area to the back door, which had obviously been broken, either by a well-placed kick or a baseball bat. Maybe even a solid brick, as the door didn't look overly sturdy.

Isaiah sighed. "I'll need to fix this."

"Now?" She frowned. "I can't sit here with key evidence. I need to turn it over as soon as possible."

"Go ahead and take it in. I'll stay here. I need to change my clothes, and it will also take me some time to get this repaired."

She rolled her eyes. "Have you forgotten the three attempts to kill you? And the fire at my place?"

"No. I have not forgotten." He turned to look at her with an intense gaze. "But I'm responsible for this building and for keeping the church a safe place for worship."

"You're risking your life to repair a door." She glared at him. "That's the most ridiculous thing I've ever heard."

Anger sparked in his eyes. "My responsibility is not ridiculous. I am here to spread the word of God. That means having a church. Besides, you can't force me to leave." He turned and headed back the way they'd come.

Grinding her teeth together in frustration, she followed.

He opened a door leading to a dark, damp basement. Flicking on the light, he headed down the stairs. She hesitated, then followed, wondering if Pinky or one of the others had been down there too.

The cobwebs didn't appear disturbed. Isaiah waved them away as he found a hammer, nails, and more wood. Without saying anything, he brushed past her to return to the main level.

To her surprise, he made quick work of the repairs. He was able to fix the door enough that it was able to be locked. After he'd finished, he stood and brushed off his hands. "That will work."

All in all, the repair hadn't taken long, making her feel small for arguing over it. She managed a smile. "May we please go now?"

He nodded, then held up a hand. "After I grab some clothes."

She waited, tapping her foot on the floor as he disappeared into his office. He closed the door behind him. When he emerged, he wore another pair of black slacks and a black shirt. "Do you own anything besides black?"

A smile quirked the corner of his mouth. "I do, but this is how people expect their church pastor to look."

She supposed he was right. Turning, she led the way back through the church. She opened the door an inch, sweeping her gaze over the area outside before stepping out.

Isaiah was close behind her, taking a moment to relock the door. She used her body as a shield the best she could, considering Isaiah was at least four inches taller than she was, to head down the stairs and to the Jeep.

She caught a glimpse of movement from the window of a house directly across the street. The residents had all been questioned, but she was fairly certain they hadn't told the police everything they knew.

The neighborhood where she'd grown up was very similar. They would rather die than be caught cooperating with the police.

She swallowed a sigh of frustration and pulled away from the curb. Her goal in joining the Milwaukee Police Department was to help eradicate crime in these types of neighborhoods. Yet it seemed impossible to crack through the tough exterior of the long-held cycle of crime and poverty.

Police work alone wasn't enough. She glanced at Isaiah, who appeared lost in thought. Maybe he was doing a good thing here. Working from the inside as one of them to be a catalyst for change.

"I admire your dedication to the church and the community." She managed a smile. "I'm sorry if I was testy."

"I understand." He met her gaze briefly, before she turned to pay attention to the road. "However, you keep forgetting one important detail in all of this."

"What's that?"

"I'm not afraid to die."

The simple statement was like a kick to the chest. She knew, of course, that those who believed, like Rhy, Joe, Brock, and Steele, among others, felt the same way. Yet hearing him say the words in such a matter-of-fact tone gave her a chill.

"Maybe you're not afraid," she agreed. "But I would think you would want more time here to help change the path some of these kids are heading down."

"Yes, that is true." He reached out to lightly touch her hand. "I didn't say I wanted to die, but that I'm not afraid. There's a difference."

Was there? Maybe. She nodded and focused on driving. It wasn't that long ago that someone had fired a shot at her squad in this same neighborhood.

Better to stay alert for danger than to think too much about her own mortality.

When they arrived back at the precinct, she quickly headed inside to find Rhy. He wasn't in his office, but she found Joe nearby.

"What do you have there?" He eyed the evidence bag curiously.

She filled him in on what she'd found. "I know this technically belongs to the third district police station, but I don't know many cops there, and honestly, there are still a few questions over what exactly went down outside the church."

"I agree with you." Joe's expression was somber. "The third district has a tough job, no question about that. But I know the mayor is very concerned about the crime in that area, especially since he raised his family there. And the fact that teens and cops exchanged gunfire is a huge red flag."

"I know." She glanced back to where Isaiah sat, his head down as he stared at the floor. "I think this is the weapon Pinky used to hold Isaiah hostage. And probably the gun that killed or wounded our officers."

"We'll put a rush on this." Joe picked up the evidence

bag. "I heard about your house fire, Rae. Where are you going to stay?"

"I haven't figured that out yet." The insurance company had informed her that they would cover temporary housing, but the amount of money didn't sound like enough to pay for a hotel. Not when she knew that it could take up to nine months to get her home repaired. "Right now, I'm focused on keeping Isaiah safe."

He tipped his head to the side. "You're welcome to stay with me and Elly. We have a new house now with a spare bedroom."

"Oh, thanks but that's not necessary." She felt herself flush. Having gotten married in February, Elly and Joe were still newlyweds, and the last thing she wanted was to impede on their privacy. "The insurance company will put me up someplace."

"Maybe you can bunk with Jina or Cassidy?" He pressed, mentioning the only other female officers on the tactical team. "I think you should consider another option too. Just in case the money runs out."

He spoke as if he knew what he was talking about, and she vaguely remembered that Colin Finnegan's wife, Faye, had her home burned down last year. Maybe Joe was right about the need to be cost conscious. She didn't have experience with this sort of thing. "I will, thanks."

"I take it the lead on Pinky didn't pan out?" Joe asked.

"No. We think he was there but was gone by the time we arrived." She hesitated, then asked, "It might be wise to put an undercover cop nearby to watch the place. Could be Pinky goes there at night."

Joe nodded thoughtfully. "I'll check with Lieutenant Marcel at the third. See what he thinks."

"And if he doesn't have the resources?" she asked.

"Then I'll follow up with the fifth district." Joe shrugged. "After hearing about your house fire, Rhy headed out to the third district to discuss how we can share resources. Captain Sanchez is supposed to be running the show, but the mayor is putting pressure on Rhy to back them up."

"That's good." She couldn't deny feeling better knowing Rhy and the rest of their team may be given more responsibility in getting to the bottom of this mess. When cops were killed in the line of duty, the lines between districts became blurred. Every cop out there wanted the person responsible behind bars.

For their own safety and that of their respective families.

"Will you let me know what Rhy decides?" She worked hard not to glance at Isaiah again. "I have a vested interest in this case."

"We all do," Joe assured her with a nod. His phone rang, and he quickly answered it. "Hey, Rhy, we were just talking about you." He listened for a minute, then glanced up at her. "Yeah, she's here with the pastor. They found a Glock in the church."

She hoped Rhy had new intel for them. She needed a distraction from the fire.

"I'll let her know, thanks." Joe disconnected from the call. "Boss wants you to meet with Mitch Callahan the arson investigator about your house fire. Then he wants you to take Isaiah back to the neighborhood to see if you can get a line on Hugo Morrison. His last-known address is a bust. There's a young family living there who claim they don't know him."

She would rather work on Hugo first but knew that the

sooner she got the conversation with Mitch Callahan off her plate, the better. "Okay, that works."

"Mitch will gladly come here," Joe added. "I'll call him now."

"Great." She smiled. "Thanks."

Mitch Callahan arrived about fifteen minutes later. "Let's talk in one of the interview rooms," Mitch suggested. "Pastor Washington, would you please join us?"

"Call me Isaiah." He quickly followed them into the interview room.

"The fire was started with gasoline as an accelerant, and it was used on multiple points of entry, which is how your house was engulfed in flames so quickly."

The news was sobering. "What about my neighbors on each side?"

"Both properties were saved, aside from some minor water damage. No one was hurt, which is a blessing. But your place is a total loss, Raelyn."

She tried not to think about how much this would cost her. Yet there was nothing she could do about that, except maybe to find a place to stay that wouldn't cost anything extra as Joe had suggested.

"I've heard about the attempts against you, Isaiah," Mitch went on. "And it sounds like you were attacked by this guy Hugo Morrison near Raelyn's place."

"Yes." Isaiah looked upset. "I feel like this is all my fault. If I hadn't decided to do some rideshare driving for extra cash, Hugo may not have spotted me at the gas station or set fire to Raelyn's home."

"You didn't light the match," Mitch said. "Although that's a good point about the gas station. We'll check the video surveillance there. Maybe we'll get a good look at this

Hugo guy if he purchased the gas from there to start the fire." Then he glanced at her. "What do you think?"

"I don't blame Isaiah; he didn't ask to be shot at and attacked." She thought for a moment. "I haven't made any enemies lately, so I have to agree that Morrison is our prime suspect for the fire."

Mitch nodded. "I know there's a BOLO out for him already." He pulled out a business card. "I have the authority to arrest him, too, so if you or anyone else on your team get a line on him, let me know and I'll be there."

She frowned, staring at the card. "No offense, but you're not a cop."

Mitch chuckled. "No, but several of my brothers are, and I've learned a lot about law enforcement over the past few years."

She was well aware the Callahans were second cousins to the Finnegans. She'd attended Joe's wedding and had met both families. She reluctantly took the card and tucked it away. "Thanks. We'll let you know if we learn anything."

Mitch nodded, then rose to his feet. "I wish there was more I could do for you, Raelyn. But if Hugo Morrison is responsible, we will prosecute him to the full extent of the law."

"I understand." She knew the arson case could be considered an attempted murder too, although that would be harder to prove. She was a witness to the first attempted murder, so it was likely that charge would trump arson. Still, she hoped the multiple murder attempts would be enough to put Morrison away for the rest of his life. It was what he deserved.

But first, they had to find him.

EVERY TIME he thought about the damage to Raelyn's home, Isaiah felt sick. No matter what she or Mitch Callahan said, he knew that her being in danger was his fault.

He stood when both Raelyn and Mitch did. He shook hands with Mitch, then followed the pair out of the interview room.

"Are you ready to hit the road?" Raelyn asked.

He nodded, as it didn't seem he had much of a choice. "What's your plan?"

"I was thinking we should head back to your place," she said, surprising him.

"There you are," another male voice said, before he could respond. Isaiah frowned when he saw Grayson.

"What's up?" Raelyn asked.

The officer arched a brow. "I was going to ask you the same thing. Joe says we're supposed to see if we can find this Morrison character." Grayson glanced at him briefly, then back to Raelyn. "I'm your backup."

"Okay." Raelyn didn't appear as disappointed as he was by the news. "I was just telling Isaiah that we should head to his house. It seems likely that Morrison, or whoever hired him, will be watching the place."

Grayson nodded. "That could work."

"Hold on." He lifted a hand. "You're both dressed in uniforms that will be easily spotted in the daylight. No one is going to come after me if they see you."

Raelyn frowned. "We're not setting you up as bait for this guy."

"Why not?" Grayson asked. Then he winced. "Sorry, I didn't mean that to sound as if I don't care about you, because I do. No offense, it's just that we need this guy behind bars ASAP."

"None taken. I agree." He was the one Hugo wanted. Why, he wasn't sure. But he did agree that it was imperative to get him behind bars.

And he'd do whatever was necessary to keep Raelyn safe.

"He has a point about the uniforms," Raelyn said thoughtfully. "We should go in plain clothes. I have one more change of clothes in my locker, then I'll have to hit a department store."

"I'm game to go in plain clothes." Grayson gestured toward the locker rooms. "Let's get changed."

The two officers left to go to their respective locker rooms. It was tempting to head off on his own but knew that would be counterproductive. Risking his life was fine if the outcome was that they were able to get Hugo in custody.

The big Black man had to have been hired by the Chief. It was the only thing that made sense. Either the Chief held a grudge from ten years ago or he'd somehow figured out that Isaiah had made the anonymous call to the third district police station.

A bit of an overkill to send Hugo after him and to torch Raelyn's home, but he knew better than most that the drug business was ruthless.

When Raelyn and Grayson returned, he found it difficult to tear his gaze from Raelyn. She was so incredibly beautiful. Even more so without her bulky uniform.

Then he frowned. "Wait. What about your vests?"

She tipped her head to the side as if surprised by his question and lightly tapped her chest. "We're wearing an abbreviated version. Don't worry, it still covers the heart."

"That's a good point, though, we should get one for the preacher." Grayson spun on his heel to grab one from the equipment room.

"He's right. I should have thought of that," Raelyn said. "Sorry."

"It's fine." He rubbed the scar on his chest again. "I guess it would be better not to have to undergo another open-heart surgery."

"Isaiah." She reached out to grasp his arm. "You don't have to do this. We can go to your place without you. Grayson doesn't have dark hair or your skin color, but we can look for an officer who is a better match to do this."

"No, it's better if I'm there." He was touched by her concern and covered her hand with his. He wanted to draw her into his arms again but knew that would not go over well with her. Raelyn would not want her fellow officers to see her as weak.

Especially since she was exceptionally strong.

When Grayson returned with the vest, Isaiah removed his shirt so he could strap it on. He caught Raelyn's somber expression when she noticed the scar, but then it was quickly covered by the stiff Kevlar.

"Thanks." He shrugged back into his shirt.

"I'll drive." Raelyn had the Jeep key fob in her hand. Grayson sighed but nodded.

They headed outside and climbed inside the vehicle. The trip to the north side didn't take long, although as always, he was keenly aware of the difference between the neighborhood he called home compared to Raelyn's ranch house.

Worlds away, he thought. And that was the stark reminder he needed to understand his secret infatuation with her was useless.

He couldn't leave this neighborhood where he had a chance to influence young lives, and no woman in her right mind would agree to live there. They didn't have a future, no matter how much he might wish for one.

Raelyn didn't drive straight to the house he rented from the mayor but took a winding route through the side streets. When she pulled into a vacant parking space, he realized she didn't want to park the Jeep in his driveway.

He couldn't blame her. Besides, his car was still there. Unless it had been stolen.

"I think we should avoid the front," Raelyn said. She turned in the driver's seat to face him. "I assume you can get us there through backyards and alleys?"

"Yes." He knew these streets better than they did. "This is a good spot. My place is only three blocks away."

"I know." She grinned. "I scoped the place out that first night I was waiting for you, remember?"

It seemed like months ago rather than two days. "Okay, you should both follow me."

Despite the fact that they were wearing casual clothes, they still looked like cops. Well, Grayson more so than Raelyn. Not just because they were Caucasian in a section of the city that was predominantly Black and Brown, but because they swept keen gazes around like cops. Moved silently and deliberately like cops.

And if you looked closely, were armed like cops.

If Hugo had someone watching the place, he figured the guy would stay back, unwilling to face the odds of three against one.

Or so he hoped.

Cutting through the backyards didn't raise an alarm. In the balmy spring air, many of the residents had their windows open. He could hear music blasting and the occasional shouting match. Most of the people around here kept to themselves.

Upon reaching his backyard, he hunkered down for a moment, glancing back at Raelyn and Grayson. He dug out his house key and held it up for them. "What do you think? Is it safe to go inside?"

"I don't know." Raelyn took the key and scowled as she looked around. "I don't like how easy it was to get here."

"You think it's possible Morrison is inside?" Grayson asked.

The comment had him looking back at his house, checking for movement. "Maybe it's better if I go in first."

"No, you're not armed." Raelyn's voice was terse. "Grayson, do you want to take the front or the back?"

"I'll head to the front," he offered. "You keep the key, use it in the back door. I'll wait to see if anyone bolts out my way. Preach, you need to stay here until we make sure it's clear."

He wanted to argue but knew it would be useless. He wouldn't put it past either of them to handcuff him in place. "Okay."

Raelyn stayed beside him as Grayson picked his way around to the front of the property. Raelyn's teammate stayed close to the house, peering around the corner cautiously before moving closer.

Isaiah could feel his stomach twist as Raelyn approached the back door. He couldn't tear his gaze away, but he silently prayed as Raelyn cautiously unlocked the door.

She pushed it in while staying back, which was a good thing when the sound of gunfire erupted from inside.

CHAPTER EIGHT

Raelyn ducked and pressed her back against the wall, hoping it was thick enough to stop a bullet. The moment the intruder stopped shooting, she listened intently, knowing she needed to be ready for the moment Grayson breached the front.

Hearing the loud thud as he kicked the front door open, she moved quickly peering around the corner into the kitchen. Hugo Morrison was inside armed with a handgun, and he made the mistake of glancing back when Grayson entered.

"Police! Drop your weapon!" Her sharp command had Morrison turning back to face her.

"You heard her," Grayson said. "Drop the gun!"

Even though Morrison was surrounded, he didn't drop his weapon. Instead, he took aim at her, leaving her little choice but to return fire.

He went down beneath the force of her shot. Grayson rushed forward to grab the gun.

"We need to clear the place." The possibility of Morrison not being there alone spurred her inside. She and

Grayson methodically cleared the entire house, exchanging grim looks before heading back down to the injured man.

Of course, Isaiah was already there, using a kitchen towel to stanch the bleeding.

"Call 911," she told Grayson, who nodded and pulled out his phone. She knelt on the other side of Morrison. "Who sent you? Why are you doing this?"

The perp's eyes remained closed, his breathing shallow. Isaiah was putting all his weight on the open wound to slow the bleeding.

"Hugo, talk to me!" She spoke louder, hoping to get a reaction. "Who sent you? Why are you trying to kill Isaiah?"

The large Black man's eyes fluttered open, and he grimaced. "Hurts."

"We have an ambulance on the way." She tried to hold his gaze, but he wasn't focused on her. He was staring at some spot over her shoulder. She resisted the urge to turn and look to make sure no one was there. "Talk to me, Hugo. What's going on here? Why are you doing this?"

Finally, he looked at her but appeared confused. As if he didn't understand the question. Then he closed his eyes and went limp.

She swallowed hard, glancing at Isaiah in horror. They couldn't lose him. They needed him alive and talking!

"Ambulance will be here any minute," Grayson said quietly.

That may be a minute too late. She reached over to check his pulse. It was faint and rapid. She was afraid he didn't have much time. "Come on, Hugo, talk to me!" She was almost begging now.

Hugo groaned, and whispered, "Chief."

She leaned forward, her pulse racing. "Who is the Chief? What's his name?"

There was no response. She looked at Isaiah again, but he shook his head helplessly, still holding pressure on Hugo's wound.

The sirens were louder now, and she knew the third district officers and the ambulance had arrived. She hated feeling so helpless. Why hadn't Hugo surrendered? Why had he pointed his gun at her, knowing he'd be shot?

As if reading her mind, Isaiah said, "I think he must be afraid of the consequences of snitching on the Chief."

"How could those consequences be worse than this?"

Isaiah's eyes darkened. "I don't know. Maybe Morrison has family somewhere, or maybe he thought dying of a gunshot wound would be better than whatever revenge the Chief might extract from him."

She shivered as the possibility. Moments later, uniformed officers entered the home, followed by two EMTs with a gurney.

Rising to her feet, she moved out of the way to make room for the medical professionals. There was nothing more she or Isaiah could do other than to pray that Hugo survived this and that they'd be able to question him when he got out of surgery.

Isaiah didn't move away from Hugo until the EMTs had him connected to their equipment and had started intravenous fluids. Then he rose and joined her in the corner of the room.

"You expected him to be inside," Isaiah murmured.

She shook her head. "Not really, but I took precautions knowing that anything was possible."

He scrubbed his face with his hands. "I was so scared watching as you and Grayson confronted him."

"We're well-trained cops," she reminded him. Although, she could understand his concern. She and Grayson acted without thinking, relying on their training to get through the tough situation.

The tactical team was the best of the best, but that didn't make them infallible. They'd lost Kyle last Christmas, although that had been a targeted attack against him rather than a random event. And yes, the team practiced different scenarios. In the end, it came down to gut instinct based on years of experience and training.

Grayson gestured for her to join him in the living room with one of the third district police officers. She and Isaiah slid past the EMT crew.

"This is Officer Mark Stern," Grayson said. "I was explaining to him how you and I were working undercover to see if we could find Hugo Morrison."

She recognized Stern as one of the cops who had responded to the church shooting. She could tell he was not happy before he spoke. "Since when do cops perform undercover work in other precincts?" he demanded.

A flash of irritation hit hard. "Shouldn't you be glad to have additional help in working the case rather than arguing over turf? I'd think you'd be more concerned with what just transpired here."

The officer flushed at her rebuke. But before he could fire back, another officer came forward, a sergeant based on the stripes on his sleeve. "I'm Sergeant O'Malley. Would you please give us your version of events?"

Gladly, she thought, trying to keep her expression neutral. The third district officers had a tough job, no question about that. But she'd think they'd welcome assistance in any form.

When Grayson nodded at her, she took the lead in

explaining how Pastor Isaiah Washington had been attacked and fired upon several times by Hugo Morrison. "We came here today in plain clothes hoping to get a glimpse of him. But we honestly didn't expect him to be waiting inside Isa—er, Pastor Washington's home."

Sergeant O'Malley's gaze slid to Isaiah for a moment, then he nodded. "Okay, so then what happened?"

"He opened fire. My partner, Grayson, breached the front door. We had him surrounded, identified ourselves as police officers, and demanded he drop his weapon." She paused, then added, "He didn't."

Sergeant O'Malley frowned at that. "Really?" There was no mistaking the doubt in his tone.

"Officer Lewis is correct," Grayson said firmly. "He knew we had him cold, but he took aim at her regardless. She fired one shot, taking him down."

She knew they'd want to take her second service weapon as evidence, so she handed it over, feeling naked without it. All she had left now was her small Smith and Wesson that fit into her ankle holster.

But there was nothing she could do about that. Rhy would place her on desk duty for sure this time, but she hoped he'd allow her to continue protecting Isaiah. Hugo was no longer a threat, but if the Chief did hire him, they were far from safe.

For all she knew, the mysterious Chief would double down on his efforts to eliminate Isaiah.

Sergeant O'Malley placed her weapon in an evidence bag. She glanced at Grayson, noticing his frown. She wouldn't reassure him about her Smith and Wesson until they were alone.

"Coming through," the EMT said.

They moved out of the way so the medical team could

get Hugo Morrison out of the house and into the waiting rig. He groaned in pain as the EMTs shifted him to get him through the broken front door.

She realized Isaiah would need to fix the front door, much the way he had repaired the break-in at the church. Hugo had intended to kill him, but why now? Isaiah has been out of jail and back in the community for years.

It all came back to the shooting that had unfolded in front of the church. But even that seemed like a strange reason to target Isaiah. It wasn't like he was out there in the middle of things. Kids and cops had exchanged gunfire.

She abruptly turned to Isaiah. "Did you ever get the list of victims' names?"

"No. And I would still like that so I can visit the families."

Yeah, she thought the list was important, too, but possibly for another reason. She looked at Sergeant O'Malley. "I would like that list of names ASAP." Reading his hesitation, she added, "I can have Captain Finnegan reach out to your Captain Sanchez if that helps. They're meeting today I believe."

O'Malley shrugged. "Fine. I'll get it for you."

"Now," she said firmly. "That list may help us figure out why Hugo Morrison risked his life to take out Isaiah."

O'Malley didn't look happy but reluctantly nodded. He headed outside to his squad, and she knew all police vehicles were equipped with computers. No printer, but these days, information could be sent and delivered electronically to phones without resorting to paper.

She and Grayson followed him out. He slid in behind the wheel and tapped computer keys. Then Sergeant O'Malley glanced at them. "You both want a list?"

"Yes, please." She needed one as she feared she'd be cut

out of the information loop. Thankfully, Grayson didn't argue.

"Emails?" O'Malley asked.

She provided hers, then Grayson did the same. It took less than a minute for the list to appear in her email folder. She tapped on her phone, opened the document, and scanned it. Five names were on the list of citizens who were killed. There was the one officer's name, too, a guy by the name of Dillon Colbert.

After forwarding the list to Rhy and Joe, she lifted her gaze to O'Malley's. "Thank you. Appreciate this."

"Yeah, sure." O'Malley waved toward the house. "I'm sorry about Stern's attitude back there. He's been taking things personally lately. He was close to Dillon."

She held his gaze, unwilling to let him off the hook so easily. "Here's the thing, we all lost a brother in blue that day. Fighting within the ranks isn't going to help. We need to work together on this, and frankly, the more cops involved with that task, the better."

"I know, I know." O'Malley lifted his hands. "I couldn't agree more."

"Good." She wanted to ask about getting fifth district officers here, too, like Reed Carmichael, but she decided that was above her paygrade. She turned away, intending to find Isaiah, knowing it wouldn't be long until the crime scene techs would be crawling around the place, searching for evidence.

"What made you ask about the list of names?" Grayson asked as they headed back to Isaiah's house.

"Maybe we're coming at this all wrong." She stopped to look at him. "The kids were shot by cops who were called in by Isaiah. He made the call anonymously, but maybe they just assumed it was him. I'm wondering if these attempts to kill him are related to family members seeking revenge."

"A possibility," he agreed. "But you'd think they'd be targeting cops, not the preacher."

"Isaiah's the one who made the call. He breached the so-called code of silence in this neighborhood." She looked around, noting the empty streets. Not a single person had come out of their homes to watch the activity. And she knew why. They didn't want to be interviewed as a witness. They didn't want to rat anyone out, and they didn't trust the police not to haul them down to the precinct if they happened to have outstanding warrants.

It was exactly what her mother had done years ago when they'd lived on the south side of Chicago. Her mother stuck her head in the sand when Kenny attacked her, pretending nothing happened.

She tried not to feel deflated. For as far as she'd come in her career, at times like this, she felt as if she was walking through quicksand, unable to make any forward progress at all.

ISAIAH HAD GONE in the basement to get supplies to fix the door, but the cranky officer, Stern, roughly took them away. "You can't touch anything. This is a crime scene."

Isaiah swallowed his protest and nodded. "Okay. But I need to fix the broken front door at some point."

"Not now" was Stern's curt response. "You need to get out of here."

And cops wondered why the community didn't trust them? It was officers with attitudes like this that gave the others a bad name.

Biting back a retort, he made his way back to the front door just as Raelyn and Grayson mounted the steps. He managed a smile. "I guess we need to stay out here."

"We'll find a place to stay soon," Raelyn said. "I'd like to show you something, though." He stepped up beside him, showing him a document on her phone screen.

His heart squeezed when he realized this was the list of victim names.

"Do any of these names sound familiar? Do they attend your church services?" Raelyn asked.

He sighed. "Two of the names sound familiar, Omar Talbert and Tyson Richards. I believe their respective mothers have attended services."

"Do you think those kids with street names are friends or relatives of these two?" She pressed. "I'm looking for another connection to investigate."

"I have no idea." He tamped down a flash of anger. "I told you I don't know the real names of those kids. They go by their street names only."

She looked thoughtful for a moment, then turned to Grayson. "We need more intel on these victims."

"I'll call Gabe Melrose," Grayson said. "I'm sure he can dig up more for us."

"Thanks." She slipped the phone back into her pocket. "I guess we can head out of here, then."

"What about the house?" Isaiah asked with concern. "I rent the place from the mayor. I can't just leave that front door broken, or there will be nothing left when I get back."

"The cops will take care of securing the place," Grayson said. "Especially if the mayor is the owner."

Maybe that's what Grayson and Raelyn would do, but not the cops here. He shook his head. "I doubt Officer Stern will lift a finger to help."

"I can change that. Hang on." Raelyn hurried back to the squad at the curb. She spoke to Sergeant O'Malley, then came back up. "O'Malley assured me he'll make sure the place is secure. He understands that he'll have to answer to the mayor if he doesn't."

Despite the dire circumstances, he couldn't help but chuckle. If the mayor didn't have enough power to get this accomplished, then no one did. "Fine. Where to?"

"Good question." Raelyn looked at Grayson. "Do you think Rhy will spring for a safe house? Or a motel?"

"Yeah, he will." Grayson didn't hesitate. "Let's head back to the Jeep. I'll call Rhy on the way."

"Good." Raelyn looked relieved, and Isaiah realized her financial situation was as tenuous as his was. Another thing they had in common.

It wasn't right that she, or Grayson for that matter, should pay out of pocket to keep him safe. Yet he wasn't sure that was the job of the police department either.

How had things gotten so complicated?

He followed Raelyn down the street to the corner, conscious of the way Grayson stayed close behind him. Even now, it was humbling to realize how these two officers didn't hesitate to put their lives on the line for him.

Was he worthy of this level of protection? Probably not. Yet he also knew God had brought them together for a reason, and it wasn't up to him to question the Lord's plan.

The trek to the Jeep was uneventful, yet Isaiah knew that people were watching them from nearby homes, peeking through blinds or around curtains. He thought about the names of the recent victims. At the very least, he wanted to visit the families of the two teenagers he'd recognized.

Yet he didn't want to place them in danger either.

They didn't cut through backyards this time. The streets were empty, which was highly unusual for this time of day. Sure, the kids should be in school, classes didn't let out until the first week of June, but no one bothered much with finding delinquent kids in this area of the city. The teachers and principals were grateful when the trouble-makers stayed home.

He highly doubted any of the kids who'd come through the church that fateful day were sitting in the classroom. Especially not Pinky.

A hint of orange movement caught his eye. He glanced at the house on the corner but didn't see anything. Had that been Tiger?

He almost mentioned the possibility to Raelyn but decided to remain silent. For one thing, there was no sign of the mixed-race kid now. And he wasn't even sure the movement had been one of the kids who'd come through his church at all.

His imagination was working overtime. Being constantly on guard was wearing on him. He didn't like looking for a gunman around every corner.

He told himself they were safe for the moment because even if the Chief did hear about Hugo being shot, it would take time for him to find a replacement.

Or so he hoped.

The rest of the trip back to the Jeep was uneventful. Raelyn slid behind the wheel, and Grayson took the passenger seat, so he climbed into the back.

"You might want to keep your head down," Grayson advised. "At least until we're out of this neighborhood."

"I live here," he felt compelled to point out.

"Yeah, and Morrison was waiting in your house with a

gun," Raelyn shot back. "It doesn't hurt to make yourself less of a target."

"I can't do my job if I stay out of sight." It was bothering him to think that some people may have come to the church to look for him because they needed someone to talk to.

"I understand." Raelyn's tone was softer now. "I know how much you care about your church and those who attend services. But you can't help them if you're dead."

He thought of the day he'd lay bleeding in the street. *It's not your time, my child.*

Was it still not his time? He had done some good here, but lately, he'd felt useless. As if God's saving him hadn't mattered much.

"Please?" Raelyn asked.

"Okay." He bent at the waist so that his upper torso was stretched out in the back seat. It wasn't comfortable, but it wouldn't take them that long to get out of the neighborhood.

There was nothing but silence for several long moments the Jeep moved through the streets. No doubt both Raelyn and Grayson were on hyperalert for any threat.

Then he heard Grayson speak. "Rhy? There was an incident at the preacher's house."

Oddly, he didn't mind the way Grayson referred to him as the preacher. He didn't sound derogatory when he said it, and that was his job after all.

"Yeah, Raelyn surrendered her weapon. I think she deserves a replacement, though. Even if you keep her off active duty, she deserves to defend herself."

Despite his deep aversion to guns, Isaiah silently agreed with that plan. Raelyn was in danger because of him. Her home had been set on fire, and she'd been nearly struck by gunfire as often as he had been.

He sent up a silent plea for God to keep her and the rest of her team safe.

"We'll be there soon," Grayson was saying now. "Ten minutes at the most."

"Where?" he asked. "To the precinct?"

"Yes," Raelyn answered. "Rhy is expecting to have more information on the Glock that was processed through the lab."

The Glock, most likely left behind by Pinky. He closed his eyes for a moment, hoping he was wrong.

"Look out!" Grayson shouted.

He almost sat up but was thrown off-balance when Raelyn wrenched the wheel hard to the left. He heard the sound of gunfire, but there was no metallic ping or breaking glass to indicate they'd been hit.

Raelyn hit the gas, the Jeep lurching forward. Then she took another series of turns, making him dizzy. After what seemed like forever but was likely only a handful of minutes, he heard Grayson say, "All clear."

"What happened?" He sat up and looked around.

"There was a car on the street with the driver's side window open," Grayson said. He turned in his seat to face him. "As we passed, I saw there was a man crouched in there with a gun. I think he was waiting for us, but thankfully, he was parked close to the intersection, so we were able to get away." He patted Raelyn's arm. "Good driving, Rae."

"Thanks." She met Isaiah's gaze in the rearview. "And that's the reason we asked you to keep your head down."

He nodded. "I get it. I'm a target."

"No lie," Grayson muttered.

He noticed the streets were changing now as they headed out of the north side of the city. Today, he was glad they were leaving the old neighborhood behind. There had to be a way to get to the bottom of this mess. He settled back in his seat when he realized they were on one of the local highways, making quick time in reaching the precinct.

As before, Raelyn drove around to the back of the building to park. He was impressed at how well she'd handled the near miss.

"We'd better check the Jeep for damage," Grayson said as he opened his door.

"Okay." Raelyn slid out from behind the wheel. He emerged from the back seat, watching as the two cops closely examined the vehicle.

"It's clear," Grayson announced.

"Let's get inside." Raelyn glanced around. "Isaiah shouldn't be out in the open like this."

Rhy was waiting for them inside, his features grim. "I noticed you were checking the Jeep."

"Someone took a shot at us but missed," Grayson said. "Raelyn got us out of there."

Rhy sighed. "This is getting out of hand."

"Do you have news for us?" Raelyn asked. "Because we could use some leads."

"Yeah." Rhy met Isaiah's gaze. "How well do you know Pinky?"

His stomach clenched. "I don't know him that well, but he has come in for services and stayed for the meal. Why?"

"That Glock left in the church was used to kill Officer Dillon Colbert and matches the slugs taken from the other two injured officers as well."

Isaiah wasn't surprised. "But we don't know that Pinky pulled the trigger. Or that it was even the gun that Pinky had used to threaten me."

"Did the lab get any prints?" Grayson asked.

"No. The weapon was wiped clean." Rhy was still holding his gaze, and Isaiah knew they believed he was protecting Pinky. And in a way he was because he absolutely did not want to see Pinky arrested for killing a cop.

If the kid entered the prison system now, he'd be changed forever, and not for the better.

____

CHAPTER NINE

Glancing between Rhy and Isaiah, Raelyn could tell her boss was about to accuse Isaiah of holding out on them. And shockingly, she wanted to jump to his defense.

"Of course, there were no prints on the weapon," she said, breaking the tense silence. "I would have been surprised if there had been."

"Where is Pinky?" Rhy asked bluntly. "And what is his real name?"

"I don't know." Isaiah's chin lifted. "I would never lie to you, Raelyn, or Grayson. I only know the fifteen-year-old as Pinky, and I don't know where he is. I do my best to befriend these kids, to provide a decent male role model. But that doesn't mean I know everything about them."

"And would you tell us if he contacted you?" Rhy pressed.

"Yes." Isaiah answered without hesitation. Then he added, "It's true that I don't want Pinky to end up in the system. I don't think jail is the place for him. But I think it would be important to get his side of the story."

"You mean the story about what happened outside the church," Raelyn said with a frown.

"We know most of that already," Rhy pointed out. "The statements from the various officers who responded to the scene are consistent. We have some general descriptions of the teens involved, but many ran off."

Including the four who'd darted inside the church, she thought with a sigh. "What about the ones who were injured and arrested?"

Rhy's expression was pained. "Three of them are still in the hospital being treated for gunshot wounds. A fourth died of complications in the hospital." At her alarmed expression, he hastened to reassure her, "Not the one you hit. He's still in the hospital, too, and according to Bax Scala, the ADA in charge of the case, we can't interview him or the others while they're medicated."

"That didn't stop the cops from questioning me ten years ago," Isaiah said.

Rhy arched a brow. "It should have." He sighed, then continued. "There's one teenager who suffered minor injuries, but he's refusing to answer more questions. His name is Max Campbell, and all we have is his initial statement, which basically accused the officers of firing their weapons first."

"Yeah, but that's only because the kids were armed," she said with exasperation. "If you draw a weapon on an officer, they're going to shoot."

"I know that," Rhy said mildly. "But Max claims no one drew a weapon until the first officer fired at them, killing the kid named Omar Talbert. They were taken aback by that and began firing in return. That's when everything went downhill." Rhy shook his head. "It's a mess. I feel bad for the Third Precinct, they're taking a lot of heat from the mayor and governor regarding the number of dead teenagers."

"I failed," Isaiah whispered. "I should have gone out to break up the drug deal myself, rather than calling the police."

"No." She put a hand on his arm. "They wouldn't have stopped the drug deal for you, Isaiah. Maybe they'd have moved to a new location, but they wouldn't have stopped."

He seemed to consider that for a moment. "Maybe not. But I didn't help the situation."

When they'd first met, she'd been so angry with him. She'd slapped handcuffs around his wrists, fully committed to hauling him down to book him for interfering in a criminal investigation. Now that she'd gotten to know him, she realized how much he truly cared about the people in his community. Especially the younger members.

The image of Pinky's resigned expression flashed in her mind. *You can't help me. No one can.*

What had Pinky done? Thinking back, he and the kids he'd been with had been off to the side when she'd come around the corner of the warehouse. They'd looked at her, then had taken off to disappear into the church. That made it highly unlikely that Pinky had been the one to shoot the cop.

Yet he'd had the Glock that killed Officer Dillon Colbert. Or so she believed. Who else but Pinky would have placed the weapon on the church altar? She doubted any of the other kids would have done that.

A big piece of the puzzle was missing, and she had no idea where to find it. She glanced at Isaiah. "Would Max Campbell talk to you?"

He shrugged. "I don't know. I'm not sure he attended any of my services so he may not know who I am."

"That's a good idea," Rhy said, his gaze filled with anticipation. "I'll call his lawyer, see if they'll agree to a meeting."

Isaiah nodded, and she knew he had doubts about the plan. But at this point, they needed to try everything. She turned to Rhy. "Hugo Morrison was taken to Trinity Medical Center. I'm hoping you can get an update on his condition in a few hours."

"I'll do my best." Rhy sighed. "I've been granted permission to pay for a hotel for you two. I have booked a suite at the City Central Hotel downtown by the courthouse under my name. If Max's lawyer agrees to a meeting, you'll be close by."

"That's fine." She frowned, exchanging a glance with Grayson. "I'm surprised Assistant Chief Michaels agreed to pay for that."

"I twisted his arm. Besides, Isaiah is on good terms with Mayor Critten, remember?" Rhy lifted his hands. "I think the City Central is better than using the American Lodge. We've caused enough damage to Gary's place over the past eighteen months. I don't want to take the risk of adding more."

"That's fine." She didn't hold out much hope that Max's lawyer would agree to a meeting. Why would he? The kid was facing enough felony charges to put him in jail for the rest of his life.

A wave of sadness hit hard. Yes, everyone had choices. She and Isaiah had both managed to drag themselves out of difficult situations. But it wasn't easy, and she was well aware that if Kenny had succeeded in his attempt to force himself on her, things may have turned out much differently.

She shied away from that thought. There was no point in

rehashing the past. She was a cop and proud of her work within the tactical team. She felt bad about shooting a kid, but he had fired at her first. The problem with these kids is that they didn't have firearm training like cops did. They got their hands on a weapon and assumed that they could fire it accurately.

Thankfully, at least for her, that wasn't the case.

"I'll make sure you can be there when they interview Morrison," Rhy said, breaking into her thoughts. "But that won't be for days yet."

If Morrison survives. Rhy didn't have to say the words they were both thinking.

"What would you like me to do?" Grayson asked.

"I'm hoping you'll continue following up on leads related to Pinky and the other kids," Rhy said. "I think Raelyn can handle watching over Isaiah for now."

She didn't like being relegated to babysitter. Granted, she'd fired her service weapon in the line of duty twice now, but that didn't mean she was content to sit this out. "There must be something I can do to help." The idea of being stuck inside a hotel suite with Isaiah for hours on end made her twitchy. She was already starting to care about him, more than she'd have thought possible.

"What about the mug shots?" Isaiah said.

She turned to him. "What about them?"

"I was able to identify Hugo Morrison, maybe there are others that I'll recognize too." He managed a grim smile. "It can't hurt. And I would like to put this entire incident to rest as much as you do."

"He has a point," Rhy agreed. "We need to work every angle possible."

"That's fine with me." She hesitated, then added, "Will you provide one of the department computers for us to use at the hotel? And ask Gabe to give us access to the database?"

"Of course. Whatever you need." His cell phone rang, and he sighed. "I need to take this. It's Captain Sanchez of the third district. I'm sure I'm going to get an earful about why you and Grayson were on their turf in plain clothes."

"Better you than me," she said. Then she walked over to the closest empty desk to grab a laptop computer. "Come on, we should head to the hotel."

"I'll talk to Gabe Melrose while Rhy's on the phone," Grayson said. "Call if you need anything."

"Thanks. We will." She still had the keys to the Jeep, so she gave Grayson a nod before making her way to the rear door, the laptop computer tucked under her arm. When she reached the door, though, she turned and handed the device to Isaiah. "Hold this." Then she removed her backup piece from her ankle holster and held it ready before stepping outside.

A quick scan of the parking lot revealed nothing alarming. Still, the threat against Isaiah was real, and she wasn't going to take any chances.

Moving quickly, she led the way to the Jeep. Isaiah followed, sliding into the passenger seat without delay. He set the laptop on the floor, then buckled in.

She drove through several side streets before heading for the interstate, keeping an eye on the rearview to make sure they weren't followed as the Jeep may have been compromised by the guy who waited in the car for them to drive by.

It wasn't likely the drug dealers on the north side had the ability to track an undercover police vehicle. Then again, she wasn't taking any chances.

Her stomach rumbled with hunger, loud enough that

Isaiah smiled. "I'm hungry too," he said. "Rosie's breakfast was amazing, but it was also hours ago."

Hours that seemed like eons. A glance at the clock indicated it was going on three thirty in the afternoon. "Okay, we'll order room service once we get to the hotel." She could have stopped along the way, but since Assistant Chief Michaels had agreed to foot the bill, she figured he could spring for a late lunch or early dinner.

"Sounds good." Isaiah stared out the window for a long moment, seeming lost in thought. "I hope going through the mug shots will provide more information related to all of this."

"Me too." She remembered what he'd said about the guy he'd worked with ten years ago, a drug dealer named Donte Wicks, and made a note to double-check that he was still in jail. It didn't seem logical that Donte would try to kill Isaiah ten years later, but if he'd recently gotten out of jail, then revenge might be a viable motive.

They arrived at the City Central Hotel a few minutes later. Isaiah carried the laptop, so both of her hands could be free. She didn't see anything alarming, though, and they were soon settled in their suite.

"Nice place," Isaiah said as he set the laptop on the small table. "I've never stayed in a hotel this nice."

"I'm with you on that one." She knew where he was coming from. Hotels were a luxury that were far out of reach for those growing up in poverty. "The DA's office tends to use this hotel for witnesses who have to testify at trial." She gestured to the window. "The courthouse is within walking distance."

"Now that's a building I'm familiar with," Isaiah said with a smile. "I went straight from the hospital to the house of corrections but had several court hearings after that."

She wanted to ask more about his incarceration, but her stomach growled again, so she grabbed the menu instead. "I'll go with the wrap. What would you like?"

"The hamburger looks good." Isaiah gestured to one of the rooms. "I need to wash up first."

She nodded and reached for the phone. After placing their order, she made quick use of the bathroom in her room as well. Surprisingly, she didn't look too awful, considering everything that had transpired that morning.

Not that her looks mattered one way or the other. Isaiah was not the man for her, no matter how nice, handsome, and caring he was. They were opposites in every way.

Shaking off the thought, she returned to the main living area. Isaiah was already there, waiting for her. "I can't log into this device."

"I know." She went over to use her police credentials to access the system. "Give me a minute to pull up the mug shots."

Gabe Melrose had given them the access she'd requested. She turned the device so Isaiah could begin going through them. "Let me know if you find anything."

"I will." He began scrolling through the photographs, his attention focused on the screen.

Swallowing hard, she tore her gaze from his profile and used her phone to see what she could find using a plain, ordinary internet search. It wasn't easy to concentrate, though. For whatever reason, she was far too aware of Isaiah.

The cop and the preacher, she thought with a silent sigh. *As if that could ever work.*

ISAIAH SCROLLED through one mug shot after another. He recognized two individuals who spent time in the drug rehab facility where he offered support as a counselor. He hadn't been an addict, but he'd done his best to use his experience of being shot and being saved by God to coach the residents in turning their lives around. Unfortunately, so many of their residents relapsed that he'd found the experience more frustrating and emotionally draining over time. He didn't think he was helping as much as he wanted to.

That was when he'd gone the route of becoming a pastor. God had saved him for a reason, and he was trying to follow God's plan. He'd thought that being a pastor would enable him to reach out to more of the people who lived around him, not just the addicts, but those who were lost, needed guidance, or who came from abusive situations, like Pinky.

But so far, he hadn't been nearly as successful as he'd hoped. Despite how he continued to pray to God for guidance.

His failure weighed heavily on his shoulders.

The soft knock on the door nearly had him jumping out of his skin. He rose to his feet, but Raelyn beat him to it, placing her eye against peephole first, then opening the door to allow the server to bring in their tray.

"Thank you," Raelyn said, providing a tip.

"Sure." The server glanced nervously at the weapon she'd left on the table.

"I'm a cop," Raelyn quickly explained. She dug in her pocket for her badge. The guy visibly relaxed.

"Okay. Please set the tray outside your door when you're finished."

Isaiah glanced at her. "You should probably put the gun back in your ankle holster."

She narrowed her gaze. "I left it out so it would be close at hand if I needed it." She gestured to the tray. "Let's eat."

Isaiah almost pressed the issue but decided that would be futile. His aversion to guns had a lot to do with being shot at close range, but he understood her need to defend herself. And him. He turned to the table and pushed the computer aside to make room for their plates. Then he took his seat and held out his hand.

After a brief hesitation, she took it. Her fingers were slender and a little cold. He held her hand gently, resisting the powerful urge to pull her into his arms.

When she glanced at him questioningly, he realized she was waiting for him to say grace. "Dear Lord Jesus, we thank You for keeping us safe in Your care today. Please continue to guide us to the truth so that those around us can be safe, especially the children in Your care. Amen."

"Amen." She gave his hand a brief squeeze. "Thanks, Isaiah. I have to admit, it does seem like God is watching over us. Well, more you than me," she added.

"Not just me," he hastened to correct her. "God is there for you, Raelyn, whenever you decide to seek Him."

She tugged her hand away to pick up her wrap. "Thanks, but I'm not sure about that."

"I am." He let her go and dug into his own meal. He wished there was a way to convince her, but he wouldn't push. She would need to make the decision for herself. He knew that if he hadn't been shot that day by Petey Dobbs and had seen the light, he wouldn't believe in God either.

He sent up another prayer that God would give Raelyn a sign of His presence, then he continued eating. He suspected all she needed was a gentle nudge.

They ate in silence for a moment. "I think that whatever happened to you ten years ago is connected to what is happening now," she said. "Are you sure you don't remember anything?"

He remembered the important part, seeing the light and hearing his grandmother's voice calling him. "I was selling dope to a rich kid named Petey Dobbs. His dad was constantly giving him money, and he used it to buy drugs. But for some reason, Daddy stopped giving him cash. When I refused to issue an IOU, he pulled a gun and shot me." He rubbed the scar on his chest. "I thought I was going to die, but then I saw a bright-white light that I know was heaven. I didn't get to go to the light the way I wanted to." He glanced at her, expecting her to scoff at the idea. Her eyes widened a bit, so he continued, "The next thing I remember was waking up in the hospital. I was awash in pain and couldn't move because the police had cuffed me to the bed."

"That must have been terrifying," she murmured.

"Yes and no," he admitted. "God wanted me to live for a reason. But I will admit, the pain of undergoing chest surgery and the subsequent recovery was not fun."

"You mentioned earlier that the cops didn't wait for you to be fully recovered before they interviewed you."

"Yeah, I remember two cops asking me questions when I could barely talk." He shook his head. "I believe they read me my rights, but I don't really remember what I told them." He shrugged. "I didn't know much, other than Petey shot me."

"But you must have mentioned your supplier and maybe even the Chief," she said thoughtfully. "I wonder if there was a doctor or nurse nearby when they spoke to you."

"I believe there was a doctor at the bedside," he said. "I remember the long white lab coat. But really, it doesn't matter if I did mention Petey Dobbs, Donte Wicks, or even the Chief. I didn't know the real name of the guy who was in charge of the drug pipeline. I was nothing more than a low-level drug dealer." It still pained him to admit how foolish he'd been.

"We need to make sure Donte Wicks is still in jail." She munched a fry. "And I wonder who those cops were. I'll see if I can get a copy of your arrest report."

"Whatever you think is best." He wasn't sure that learning the names of the cops who'd questioned him would help, but Donte Wicks could be holding a grudge against him.

Raelyn pulled the computer closer. She stuck a fry in her mouth, then did a simple case search on Donte Wicks. There were a few of them in the system, but he knew Donte was only a few years older than he was.

"This one." He pointed at the screen.

She clicked on the case to see that Donte Wicks had been sentenced to ten years in prison for attempted murder. He hadn't paid much attention before, but now he noticed that the arrest was five weeks after he'd been shot.

"I'm sure he's still doing time." He straightened and took another bite of his burger. "I highly doubt Donte was nice enough during his incarceration to earn an early release for good behavior."

"Yeah, but I think the time frame is close enough that he might be up for parole regardless. The court records aren't always as up to date as we'd like." She pulled out her cell phone to make a call. "I'll have Gabe Melrose dig into that possibility."

"Okay." He finished his burger and fries while she made the call to her tech guy. All this talk of prison made him extra grateful for the meal before him. Prison food was awful, bland, and tasteless. Sometimes unrecogniz-able to the point where he'd suspected the mystery meat had been left out overnight on purpose to make them suffer.

That was the main reason he'd learned how to cook.

His thoughts must have been reflected on his face because Raelyn surprised him by resting her hand on his arm. "I'm sure that was a terrible time for you."

"Yeah." He didn't like talking about it. There was nothing more terrifying than being targeted by a group of inmates. Which he had been on several occasions. He shied away from that thought.

"You mentioned selling drugs because you needed money." She seemed anxious to understand.

"Yes. As I mentioned, my ma was sick and lost her job. We were one step away from being out on the street." He turned to meet her amber gaze. "I know it was stupid to take the easy way out, but at eighteen, it seemed the simple solution."

"I can imagine." She finished the last of her fries and pushed her plate away. "Although I get the impression your mother wouldn't have approved."

He winced because she was right. "No, she wouldn't have. I lied and told her I got a great job. She was too sick and weak to press for details."

She nodded thoughtfully at that. "Maybe she didn't want to know."

"Maybe she didn't," he agreed. He finished his food, too, and then stood to place their dirty dishes on the tray. "Although I'm sure she learned the truth after I was shot."

"Did you get to see her in the hospital?" she asked.

"Nope. Prisoners don't get visiting privileges. They told me I had to wait until I was discharged and sent to the house of corrections." That rule had rankled the most. It seemed cruel and inhumane, although one of the nurses had told him it was a safety risk because some prisoner patients in the past had used family members to get busted out of the hospital. "The worst part was learning that my ma died when I was incarcerated. She'd been sick before and relapsed after I was shot."

She sucked in a harsh breath. "Oh, Isaiah. I'm so sorry."

"Yeah, me too." He managed a weak smile. "I held a lot of anger in my heart over that. The jail pastor helped me work through it, but even now, I still miss her."

She stood and wrapped her arm around his waist. "At least you know your mother loved you. That's the most important thing of all."

He hugged her as the words registered. "Are you saying you didn't have that?"

"Not even close." Her tone was light, but he could see the dark anguish in her gaze. "My mother lied to the police to protect her boyfriend, Kenny, who tried to sexually assault me." She rested her head on his shoulder. "That was when I understood she cared more about him than me. When the state pulled me out of there, I think she was glad to be rid of me."

Dear Lord Jesus, he thought, pulling her close. What mother would do such a thing? Then again, Pinky's father had slammed a hammer down on a young boy's hand to punish him.

He knew better than most that people could be monsters.

"I don't know what to say," he whispered. "Other than I believe God spared you from being assaulted. And I'm in awe of how you changed your life for the better."

She nodded, still leaning her head against his chest. He didn't mind. He wanted nothing more than to hold her close.

And to kiss her.

As if sensing the sudden tension that coursed through him, she moved closer and tipped her head back. He stared at her mouth, imagining how soft and sweet it would be. But he didn't dare make a move, unwilling to make her feel uncomfortable.

"Raelyn." His voice came out a strangled whisper.

She searched his gaze, then smiled. His heart squeezed as she lifted up onto her tiptoes to kiss him.

That was all the encouragement he needed. He gathered her close, reveling in their embrace. He eagerly deepened their kiss, the taste of her going straight to his head, making him dizzy. He wanted her. Needed her. Maybe even loved her.

Despite their differences, he was falling for Raelyn in a big way.

CHAPTER TEN

Kissing Isaiah was amazing. But all too soon, reality seeped into her brain. She broke off from the kiss, resting her forehead on his chest for a moment to steady herself before stepping back out of his arms.

"I—uh." She had no idea what to say. She honestly wasn't sorry for kissing him. "This probably won't work," she finally said. "I'm obviously attracted to you, but that's not enough."

A half smile tugged at the corner of his mouth. "I'm obviously attracted to you, too, and that is enough. Other things can be worked out."

Could they? A flare of hope lightened her heart, but then she ruthlessly crushed it out. "I don't think so. There's too much we don't agree on. Let's just focus on being friends, okay?"

There was a flash of hurt in his blue eyes, but he nodded. "Of course. I'll always be your friend, Rae."

The way he used the shortened version of her name made her silly pulse kick up again. What was wrong with her? She didn't do things like this. Kissing a pastor? Really?

"We need to get back to work." Lame as the excuse might be, it was the best she could do. And for a moment, she couldn't remember what they'd been working on prior to this.

Her fault. She shouldn't have told him about her mother. About her childhood. Was he right about God sparing her from being raped? Maybe.

She tried to clear her mind from that amazing kiss. One she'd initiated. She gave herself a mental shake.

Donte Wicks and mug shots. That's what they'd been working on. Edging past Isaiah, she returned to the computer, logging back in and pulling up mug shots. Then she did a search to get Donte's jail photo up on the screen.

Isaiah came up beside her, so close she could feel the warmth radiating from him. She forced herself to examine Donte's features. "This is the guy who you worked for, right?"

"Yeah. That's Donte." Isaiah tapped the screen. "But the scar above his left eyebrow? That's new. Well, not new as it doesn't look fresh but must have happened before his arrest nearly ten years ago."

She nodded, wondering if the attack that had left a scar was part of the reason Donte was seeking revenge. There was absolutely no evidence of Donte being involved in hiring Hugo Morrison, but it was one working theory.

The other theory was that the Chief, whoever that was, had hired Hugo Morrison.

"I wonder how Donte got arrested," Isaiah said, as he dropped into the chair at the table. "It looks like that didn't happen until five weeks after I was shot. I was at the house of corrections by then. I was only in the hospital for two weeks. And I never gave up his name, at least not that I remember."

"Maybe Gabe can get Donte's arrest report too." She turned away to text Gabe, desperate for something to do. The idea of spending the rest of the afternoon and evening with Isaiah made her antsy. They'd been spending too much time together. She would ask Grayson to swap places with her, but she was on administrative duty after shooting Morrison. Grayson and the others were on full duty and more valuable to the team.

"I'll keep going through the mug shots," Isaiah said.

"Thanks." She paced the length of the living area, wishing Gabe would get back to her. And that Isaiah would find something for them to go on. There had to be something behind these attacks.

When her phone rang, she almost wept with relief when she saw Gabe Melrose's name on the screen. "What do you have for me?"

"I'm sending you the arrest reports for Isaiah Washington and Donte Wicks," he said. "And I was also able to find out that Wicks has been out on parole for the past ten days."

"You're kidding." What were the chances of that? First Donte Wicks gets out on parole, then the attacks against Isaiah begin. "He could be the one who hired Hugo Morrison."

"Maybe, although I'm not sure where he would have gotten the cash to hire a hit man," Gabe said. "Seems more likely he'd do the deed himself."

That was true, but the timing was too much of a coincidence. "Thanks, Gabe. I need the name and address of Donte's parole officer. Meanwhile, I'll check out those reports."

She heard him sigh, but he simply said, "Got it."

"He's really out on parole, huh?" She turned to see

Isaiah looking at her. "I have to admit I'm surprised I haven't seen him hanging around the old neighborhood."

"Maybe he was avoiding your church." She shrugged. "I really think he's a part of this. We don't know that Morrison is the one who took a shot at you from the abandoned warehouse. Maybe that was Wicks."

"No, they'd have come for me together," Isaiah said. "And with two against one, they'd have already succeeded in taking me out."

She shivered at the thought of losing him. Then reluctantly agreed with his assessment. "Okay, so Morrison is the shooter. He's working either on behalf of Wicks or the Chief."

"Wicks just got out, so I don't see how he can have enough money to pay Morrison. Even if he was able to slide back into the drug trade, ten days isn't enough time to make that kind of money."

And he would know, she realized. "Yeah. I hear you. I still want to talk to Wick's parole officer. Maybe he can fill in the gaps."

"Donte would need a stable address and a job," Isaiah said thoughtfully. "That's a condition of being on parole."

"We can get that information from the parole officer too." She was relieved to have something to focus on. "There may be time today to get over there."

"By five?" Isaiah frowned. "That only gives us a hair over twenty minutes."

"Let's head out to the Jeep. You can bring the laptop along." She pulled the key fob from her pocket and took a moment to tuck her weapon into her ankle holster. "I'll call Gabe on the way."

"Fine with me." Isaiah rose and joined her at the door. They left the suite and hurried outside. Large clouds had rolled in, bringing the threat of a May thunderstorm. She hoped the weather would hold off for a while yet.

She called Gabe once they were seated. "I need that parole office address," she said. "We want to get there before they shut down for the day."

"Cool your jets, Rae. I was working on that," he said with a hint of exasperation. "Okay, here goes." He rattled off the address. She glanced at Isaiah who was nodding as he listened.

"I know where it is," he said. "Thanks, Gabe."

"Anything else?" There was a hint of sarcasm in his tone.

"No, but thank you." She ended the call, refusing to feel guilty. Gabe would get over it, and they were on a tight timeline. She glanced at Isaiah. "Where to?"

"It's the same parole office I had. Take the interstate to Locust. I'll tell you from there."

"Got it." She headed north. "I hope the traffic isn't too bad."

He didn't say anything more, other than giving her directions on where to turn. Thankfully, they arrived at the parole office with five minutes to spare.

She jumped out from behind the wheel and hurried inside with Isaiah. The short, heavyset African American parole officer was shrugging into a light raincoat. He glared at them. "We're closed. Come back tomorrow."

"I'm MPD officer Raelyn Lewis." She pulled out her badge. "I know it's time for you to leave, but I need five minutes."

"I'm done for the day." He didn't seem to care about her status as a cop. "Come back tomorrow."

"Officer Ragland?" Isaiah stepped forward. "Do you

remember me? Isaiah Washington? You were my parole officer too."

The officer narrowed his gaze, then slowly nodded. "Yeah, I do remember you. It's been a long time."

"Eight and a half years," Isaiah agreed. "There have been several attempts to kill me over the past few days. We would like to know Donte Wicks home address and place of employment to make sure he's not involved."

To her surprise, Officer Ragland's eyes gleamed with anticipation. "Oh yeah? You think Donte has come after you?"

"Yes, sir." Isaiah smiled. "That should only take one minute, and then we'll be on our way."

"Fine." Officer Ragland stomped toward the desk and sighed loudly as he logged back in. She found herself holding her breath as he pulled up the information. He scribbled notes on a sticky note, then logged off the computer and shut it down. "Here." He handed the note to Isaiah rather than to her. "Donte is supposed to be living with his aunt Corrine Lorry. Let me know if you find out he's responsible for those attacks against you."

"We will," Raelyn said, trying to take control of the situation. "I'm sure it won't take much to revoke his parole."

"Drugs, a weapon, or missing too much work," Officer Ragland agreed. "I hope you get to arrest him. He's a bad dude," Ragland added with a dark frown.

"Thanks again." Isaiah turned to the door, giving her a look that implied she should follow. She would have rather grilled Officer Ragland for more information regarding Donte Wicks and why he considered the guy to be dangerous but told herself to be satisfied with getting the addresses.

They could always come back the following day if needed.

"Yes, thank you." She followed Isaiah outside and lowered her voice. "I'm a little surprised the same parole officer is here after all this time."

"I'm not." He arched a brow. "It's not as if being a parole officer is a lot of work. They do their follow-ups as told, and if someone doesn't show, they call the police. They're paid by the state and have state benefits, including a decent pension. They can retire after twenty-five years with a full pension. I'm sure Ragland only has a few years to go before he's done with this job forever."

She scowled and yanked the Jeep door open. "You make it sound as if that's the goal for all cops."

"Not all, but many." He flashed a smile. "You're one of the good ones, Raelyn. And I know there are others. But I've come across some apathetic officers too."

She didn't want to admit he was right about that because she'd seen some of those same officers. In her opinion, there weren't that many who were just going through the motions, but even one in ten was too many. She changed the subject. "Let's head to Donte's aunt's home address first."

He nodded in agreement, and they both slid into the Jeep. She sat for a minute, waiting for him to pass over the note.

"Interesting. This is only eight blocks from your church." They'd caught Hugo Morrison red-handed at Isaiah's home, but she couldn't help but think Donte was involved in some way too. "I'd be surprised if he didn't know you were the pastor there."

"I don't think Donte cares about church one way or the

other, much less who performs the services each Sunday," he said mildly.

"But you serve free meals, and that's the sort of thing that gets noticed." She didn't bother to hide her exasperation.

He could downplay Donte's involvement all he wanted, but she knew better. Donte Wicks likely discovered Isaiah Washington was the church pastor. One thing about these sorts of neighborhoods. People might pretend there's nothing bad going on, but they also knew far more about what happened around the neighborhood than they were willing to admit to.

This place wasn't much different from the south side of Chicago. High crime rates, a deep distrust of the police, and the unwillingness to talk to outsiders.

Yeah, she knew full well there were plenty of hidden secrets here. She could only hope they'd get some intel from Donte Wicks himself.

Or evidence of a parole violation so she could toss him back in jail.

ISAIAH DIDN'T WANT to admit how shocked he was to discover Donte lived so close to the church. If not for catching Hugo Morrison in the act of shooting at Raelyn, he'd have been certain Donte was responsible.

He must have given up Donte's name when he was a patient at Trinity Medical Center. And those officers had used that intel to find and arrest Donte. They would have had to catch him in the act, since no one had bothered to come and take his formal statement about Donte's role in the drug-running operation. And they likely couldn't use his statement in a court of law since he'd been under the influence of pain medications.

He swallowed hard and concentrated on scanning the neighborhood, searching for a threat. It was past five o'clock now and the place that Donte was working was a small manufacturing company that he doubted worked past five.

Either Donte would be home or he'd arrive there soon. Part of being on parole was wearing an ankle monitor. Not that those monitors were foolproof because they were only as good as the people watching them.

And he knew the so-called monitoring wasn't real time. Instead, the data would be downloaded, and then an arrest warrant would be issued. That took time and resources.

Five minutes later, Raelyn pulled up in front of a house that was dark. With the clouds swirling overhead, the houses around them had lights on inside.

But not this one, where Donte's aunt Corrine lived.

"Doesn't look promising," Raelyn said, throwing the gearshift into park and killing the engine. "But let's knock anyway. Maybe she's sleeping."

He reluctantly slid out to join her on the sidewalk. He didn't like being out in the open like this. Maybe the threat of rain would keep people in their homes.

Together, he and Raelyn mounted the steps to the house. It was in better shape than some of them, which may be why the parole board allowed Donte out in the first place. Raelyn knocked at the door, but there was no response.

He leaned in, listening intently. Still there was nothing. Not the sound of a muted TV or even a radio.

She tried again, with the same result. With a grimace, she turned and headed back to the Jeep. "Let's wait here for a few minutes. See if anyone comes home."

"If you're going to do that, we should park farther down the street." He slid into the passenger seat. "This is too obvious. If Donte sees the Jeep, he's likely to avoid coming home."

"Then he'd be in violation of his parole," she said.

He shook his head. "It's not enough. He could come up with a million excuses. The bus was late, or the traffic was bad, or the weather."

"Okay, okay. I'm moving." She started the engine and drove down the street. Then she made a U-turn to park on the opposite side of the road with a decent view of Aunt Corrine Lorry's house.

Then she shut down the engine again and sat back. "Patience isn't my strong suit," she muttered.

"Really? I never would have guessed."

She let out a low chuckle. "Yeah, well, I'm working on it."

He glanced at her, remembering with far too much clarity the impact of their kiss. The one she said shouldn't have happened.

The one where she made it clear that while she might be attracted to him, there would never be anything more between them.

He wanted to hold her close and to kiss her again. The more time they spent together, the more he realized how much they had in common. They'd both suffered difficult childhoods but had pulled themselves out of the gutter to make something of themselves. She'd gone through more than he had considering what her mother had done. He had only seen the light, literally, after being shot and nearly killed by Petey Dobbs.

Raelyn was an amazing woman.

And she wanted nothing to do with him.

Maybe it hurt a bit, but he'd get over it. He could handle rejection; it wouldn't be the first or likely the last. Shondra had left him for Beau, which had burned deep. Yet what bugged him the most was that Raelyn was ignoring the fact that the chemistry between them was off the charts. That they had something special that deserved a chance to grow into something more.

If she had the courage to let it.

"Is that Donte?" Her question pulled him from his thoughts.

At that moment, large drops of rain hit the windshield, making it difficult to see clearly. He leaned forward, trying to get a clear view of the guy walking down the street, a hoodie pulled up against the rain and no doubt to hide his features.

"Maybe." He glanced at her. "Should we get out and approach him?"

"Not yet." She kept her gaze on the rain-splattered windshield. "Let's see if he goes into Aunt Corrine's house."

The hoodie guy was walking fast, and sure enough, he turned to mount the stairs to his aunt's house.

Raelyn started the Jeep but turned the automatic headlights off as she pulled forward. Donte disappeared inside.

"Let's go." She killed the engine and slid out, ignoring the rain pelting them from the sky. Together, they ran up to the front door of Corrine Lorry's home. There was a slight overhang above the door that offered some protection from the rain.

There was a light on inside now. Raelyn knocked on the door, then hit the doorbell. There was no responding ringing sound coming from inside when she did so, making him think the doorbell was broken.

No one came to the door.

Raelyn knocked again, harder this time. "Donte Wicks! It's the police! Open up!"

Instantly, the light flicked off. Not a good sign.

Stubbornly, she thumped on the door again. "Police! Open up!"

Still nothing, and the tiny hairs on the back of his head lifted in alarm. All parolees knew they were supposed to cooperate with the police. It was another rule governing their ability to stay out of jail.

"Maybe that wasn't Donte," he said. "We couldn't see his face."

"You think Aunt Corrine has a bunch of guys living here?"

"No, but that doesn't mean she doesn't have a son of her own living here." He glanced around the deserted street, wishing they had more protection. "Let's go. We can come back tomorrow. Or meet up with Donte at work."

She shot him a frustrated glance, but then reluctantly nodded. "Okay, but I'm going to ask Rhy to issue a search warrant."

"This isn't your district, remember?" He couldn't explain why he was on edge. The rain didn't help. "Let's go. I think it's best if we get out of here."

"We came to talk to Donte Wicks," she said in protest. But then she turned and headed back down the stairs to the street.

"We know where he lives. And where he works." He quickly followed her down. "That was worth the trip. And he's home, so we know he's not out on the street selling drugs."

She didn't look convinced. And he couldn't blame her. He wouldn't put it past Donte to slip out later and do some drug dealing on the side.

That gave him an idea. He waited until they were both in the Jeep before turning to face her. "If Donte is selling drugs, he won't be out where the ankle monitor can be tracked. He'd have people coming to him."

Her expression brightened. "Of course, that makes perfect sense. I should have considered that for myself."

The thought hadn't entered her mind since she had never worn an ankle monitor. He almost said that the crook and the cop made a great team but decided that pointing it out would not help his case.

Raelyn drove the Jeep around the block, still keeping the headlights off, which made it even more difficult to see in the rain. She went slow, though, and soon they were back in their position along the opposite side of the road.

"I'm not sure they'll go to the front," she said, tapping her thumbs on the steering wheel. "I may have to go out back to watch the side door."

"No, I don't think that's a good idea." He tried to hide his alarm. "Let's just give it a few minutes, okay? No reason to get soaked more than we already are."

She frowned but didn't argue. They had each of their windows open an inch to keep the air flowing through. His damp clothes added a chill, but he ignored the discomfort.

He secretly hoped she'd get tired of sitting here and would decide to head back to the City Central Hotel. There was no reason for them to stick their necks out like this.

They could interview Donte tomorrow. He knew that being in this neighborhood after dark was not smart, especially for a woman.

A long silence stretched between them as they both remained focused on Aunt Corrine's house. The light had not come back on, which he found curious. Either Donte had seen the Jeep and suspected they were there for him, or he was just being extra cautious.

Maybe both.

There was no activity on the street either. The rain continued to pummel the earth, creating small rivers of water streaming down the sloped street.

"This isn't going to work," Raelyn finally said with a sigh.

He was about to agree when he heard two muffled pops.

Gunfire? From inside Corrine Lorry's house?

"Stay here." Raelyn pulled her weapon from her ankle holster, then slid out of the car. "Call 911 and request backup for possible gunfire."

"Wait! You can't go in there alone!" He used his disposable phone to dial 911 as Raelyn ignored his plea and rushed toward the house. After making the call to the dispatcher, letting her know Raelyn was on scene and needed backup, then he slipped the phone into his pocket and rushed out into the rain to follow her.

"Police!" Raelyn shouted, her voice muted by the rain. She tried the door, but it was locked. Then she kicked it with her foot.

It still didn't move. He came forward to help when he saw a dark shape near the corner of the house.

"Down!" He threw his arms around Raelyn, taking her down to the porch as more gunfire rang out. Then the sound stopped as abruptly as it had started.

The shooter was getting away!

"Get off me." Raelyn pushed at him. "We need to get inside."

He released her, managing to stand. Then he checked the door. The jam was broken, but the door didn't swing free. He kicked it for her, and this time it swung open.

"Me first." Raelyn pushed ahead of him, reaching for the light switch along the wall.

A lone lamp in the corner of the room flicked on. The prone figure of a man was sprawled on the floor face down. Even from the doorway, he could see the dark bullet holes on the back of the fallen man's T-shirt and blood was pooling beneath him. Isaiah rushed forward dropping to his knees and searching for a pulse.

There was nothing. He moved the man's head enough to see his face. Donte Wicks, down to the scar above is eyebrow.

Whoever had shot him had done so to make sure Donte would never talk to the authorities ever again.

CHAPTER ELEVEN

Raelyn swallowed a wave of frustration as she listened to the sounds of approaching sirens. She should have pushed for a search warrant. Should have continued hammering on the door until Donte had answered. Should have found a way to get inside under exigent circumstances.

Now their only lead was gone. Shot dead in his aunt's home.

Because of her. The timing was too much of a coincidence. She had to believe the shooter had recognized the Jeep and had killed Donte because they were sitting outside waiting to talk to him.

Isaiah came over to stand beside her. For not being a cop, he'd been careful not to disturb the crime scene. Other than to make sure Donte didn't need medical care. She drew him toward the door.

"We should wait outside." As they stood on the porch, huddling beneath the overhang to escape the worst of the rain, she could see the red-and-blue flashing lights as two squads approached. "I didn't see any drugs lying around. I believe he was shot to keep him from talking to us."

"I agree. Although he could have drugs in his pockets or stashed in a hidey-hole somewhere." Isaiah smiled grimly. "Most dealers are smart enough not to leave them in plain sight."

He would know. She nodded and drew in a deep breath as the officers emerged from their respective vehicles. The downpour had passed, leaving a light drizzle in its wake. She nearly groaned when she recognized Officer Mark Stern. His eyes narrowed with anger when he recognized her too.

"You again?" he demanded. "Why are you sticking your nose in our business?"

She kept her voice level with an effort. "I came to talk to Donte Wicks about Hugo Morrison, the man who tried to shoot me. Unfortunately, Donte didn't answer the door. We were just sitting in our vehicle deciding our next steps when we heard the gunfire." She arched a brow. "Did you expect me to just sit there and wait for you?"

"You shouldn't be here at all," Stern snapped.

"And you should be happy to have additional help," she shot back. "This is the city's highest crime area after all."

"What are you insinuating?" Stern took a step toward her. "That we're not doing our jobs?"

"If you don't mind, there's a dead man inside," Isaiah said in a calm, yet steely tone. "You may want to focus on him?"

She didn't back down, holding Stern's gaze. His partner seemed annoyed by Stern's attitude and edged past him to head inside.

Stern finally turned to follow. She really had no idea why Stern was being a jerk, then again, their tactical team was called in for situations that took place around the entire city, so she didn't have a home turf so to speak.

Yet she couldn't imagine getting angry over another cop helping out.

"Remember, his fellow officer was killed during the initial shoot-out," Isaiah said in a low voice.

"So he blames the tactical team because we didn't prevent his friend's death?" She scoffed. "That makes no sense. He and the others responded to this area first. We were sent to back them up."

"No one said grief was logical," Isaiah said with a shrug.

He was playing the role of peacemaker, and she irrationally found that annoying. But she supposed that was his nature, while hers was to confront and argue. More proof of how completely opposite they were.

"Whatever. I still think he's being a jerk." She headed inside to hear what was being discussed.

"Two slugs in the back from close range." Stern's partner, Officer Turner, was crouched near Donte's dead body. "We'll have to wait for the detectives to get here, to go through his pockets for drugs."

She wondered if she should mention that her presence here may have caused this. But the moment was lost when Sergeant O'Malley and two detectives arrived on the scene.

"You again?" O'Malley looked more surprised than angry. "I thought you were on administrative duty."

"I am. Sort of." She wondered if Rhy would be upset at her being here too. That bothered her more than Stern's annoyance. She was loyal to Rhy, Joe and the rest of the team. The last thing she wanted was to create issues. "We only came to talk to Donte Wicks, that's all. He never answered the door. We were in the Jeep deciding our next steps when we heard the gunfire. That's when we broke in to enter the premises." She gestured to the busted door frame. "We found him lying on the floor, dead."

"I knew Donte Wicks from the past," Isaiah added helpfully. "I thought he might open up to me."

O'Malley sighed, then nodded. "Fine. You'll have to give your statements to Detective Walling, and then I'd like you both to leave. We'll take it from here."

The female detective stepped closer. "I'm Olivia Walling."

In the spirit of full cooperation, Raelyn started at the beginning, stopping in at the parole office and then coming here. She didn't get the same level of animosity she experienced with Stern. "We heard the gunshots and ran inside."

"I saw a dark shadow leaving, and that person fired at us," Isaiah added. "But with the rain, I didn't get a good look at him. Or her."

Detective Walling smiled at Isaiah. She was attractive, and for the first time, Raelyn felt a tiny spurt of jealousy. Which was ridiculous since she and Isaiah were just friends.

What about that bone-melting kiss? She gave herself a mental shake. Enough already. She had no claim on Isaiah one way or the other. If he wanted to see Detective Walling again, that was his prerogative.

"There's no sign of a forced entry in the back," an officer announced, coming from around the corner. Water dripped from the brim of his hat. "Either the door was left open or the vic knew his killer."

"No one leaves their doors unlocked here," Isaiah said.

"He's probably right," Walling agreed. The detective eyed them both for a moment, then put her small notebook away. "You're both free to go. We'll be in touch if we need anything more."

"Thanks." Raelyn gestured for Isaiah to follow her to the Jeep. She thought it was interesting the detective didn't separate them for the interview, but maybe that had been done out of professional courtesy as she was a fellow cop.

"Back to the City Central Hotel?" Isaiah asked once they were seated. She turned the heat up to help dry their wet clothes.

"Yes." She couldn't hide her depression over the way this trip had turned out. "Unless you have another idea?"

"I wish I did." He looked just as dejected. "I had hoped to convince Donte to work with us on identifying the Chief. I assume that same man hired both Donte's killer and Hugo Morrison."

She thought about that for a moment as she pulled away from the curb and headed downtown. "I wonder why Donte wasn't killed in jail. If the Chief was worried about Donte leaking his true identity, why wait until now?"

He frowned. "I don't have a good answer for that, other than it's not as easy to arrange a jail hit as TV shows make it out to be."

"I've seen it happen." It was only two months ago that several men in custody were killed before they had a chance to cooperate with the authorities. "But that was in the Milwaukee County jail, with help from an insider. Not the state prison."

"Or the house of corrections," Isaiah said.

She lapsed into silence, her thoughts going over what little they knew. Hugo Morrison and Donte's killer must lead back to the Chief. And if that was the case, the security around Hugo Morrison needed to be tightened. Using the hands-free function, she called Rhy. She needed to tell him the latest news anyway.

Steeling herself for his wrath, she braced herself when he answered her call. "What's going on, Rae?"

"I'm sorry to bother you at home." She winced, realizing

the hour was past seven o'clock at night. She could hear the sound of baby Colleen babbling in the background. "This can wait until tomorrow if that's better."

"Spill it," Rhy demanded. "I sense you have bad news."

"I do." She glanced briefly at Isaiah, who nodded encouragingly. "We just left the north side of Milwaukee. Unfortunately, Donte Wicks was murdered."

There was a long moment of silence from Rhy, and she feared he'd suspend her.

"We went to the parole office to get the most recent address for Donte Wicks, as he was just let out on parole. We only wanted to talk to him; Isaiah knows him from the past. He never answered the door, so we were going to leave. We were in the Jeep when we heard two gunshots. We kicked in the door and found him dead on the living room floor." The words came out in a rush as if the mere explanation could get her off the hook.

But then she realized how often she used the word *we* and nearly groaned. Isaiah wasn't a fellow cop. If she'd been thinking straight, she'd have asked Grayson to ride along.

"I'm sorry," she finally said. "Isaiah thought he could convince Donte to talk to us. But the more important reason I'm calling is that I'm concerned about Hugo Morrison. He needs to be well protected while he's in the hospital."

"This is your idea of sitting in a hotel room looking at mug shots?" Rhy sounded exasperated. "You shouldn't have tried to talk to Donte Wicks alone, Raelyn. Isaiah doesn't count."

"I know. It's just that they have a history." She tightened her grip on the steering wheel. "I will understand if you suspend me from the team."

"I won't do that, but you need to follow orders," Rhy said calmly. "You're on administrative duty, the exemption from that was only for the initial shooting event, not the recent altercation with Morrison. And if you do something like this again, you will be suspended, understand?"

"Yes, sir." She appreciated the way Rhy was cutting her a break. "Thank you. We'll stay at the hotel. But I still think you need to place the officer sitting on Morrison on high alert. I have no doubt that Wicks was shot to keep him from cooperating with us."

"I'll recommend a second officer," Rhy agreed. "Anything else?"

"No, sir." As much as she wanted to be there when they interviewed Morrison, she was in no position to ask for a favor. "Again, I'm sorry to bother you."

"Get some sleep, Rae. You've been through a lot."

"I will. Good night." She ended the call.

"He cares about you," Isaiah said.

"He does, but he won't continue to put up with me breaking the rules." She knew Rhy and Joe were tough but fair. "It doesn't matter since we have nothing more to go on anyway."

"I feel guilty over Donte's death," Isaiah confided. "As if our going there put a target on his back."

"I know. I feel the same way." She sighed, then added, "But someone within law enforcement would have had to talk to him sooner or later. I hate to say this, but I doubt he'd have lived long either way."

"You may be right about that. The initial shooting was just two days ago, so that may have been the catalyst," Isaiah said. "And that road leads back to me too. The Chief must assume that I'm the one who called the cops that day."

"Maybe." She really didn't know what to think. They rode the rest of the way in silence, each lost in their thoughts. The City Central Hotel parking lot was only half full, and she chose a spot near the side entrance.

"This way." She led Isaiah through the side door and to their suite. Their feet made squishing sounds on the tile as they walked. The tray they'd left outside the room had been removed by the hotel staff. She used the key and pushed the door open, waiting a minute and peeking into the room cautiously first, before heading inside.

Everything appeared as they'd left it. Which made sense. There wouldn't be any housekeeping services offered until the morning, and she would make sure to decline them, anyway.

"Would you like me to keep searching mug shots?" Isaiah asked.

"There's no need to do that now." The attacks on Isaiah nagged at her. She was convinced the Chief had killed Donte, and it was only a matter of time until someone tried to get to Isaiah again. She forced a smile. "It's early, but I'm going to call it a night." Her clothes were wet, and his were too. They'd need to dry out before the morning.

"I think that's a good idea." Isaiah smiled wearily. "Rhy is right about the fact that you've been through a lot. I think we both deserve some rest. Good night, Raelyn."

"Good night." She wanted to hug and kiss him but forced herself to turn away. Her emotions were all over the place and living in close quarters with Isaiah wasn't helping.

She hung her damp clothes in the bathroom and crawled into bed. But despite her fatigue, sleep didn't come easily. For the first time ever, she prayed for God to watch over them.

Especially Isaiah.

ISAIAH SAW Donte's dead body every time he closed his eyes. But after several prayers, sleep claimed him. When he awoke next, early morning sunlight was shining between the curtains.

After getting dressed in his thankfully dry but badly wrinkled clothes, he went in search of coffee. He was surprised Raelyn wasn't already out there, but quickly made a pot for them to share.

As the coffee brewed, he went back to the computer. He logged in, having caught and remembered Raelyn's password, and found Donte's face staring at him from the screen. There was nothing he could do now but move on. Donte had done his time and hadn't deserved to be murdered.

But it wasn't up to Isaiah to question God's plan.

When the coffee was finished, he rose to fill a cup. The door to Raelyn's room opened, so he reached for another cup. "Coffee?"

"Thanks." She looked beautiful as always. He wasn't sure why his senses responded to her like this. He hadn't lived the life of a monk, but he hadn't dated a lot since Shondra either, mostly because he hadn't been very interested.

Not the way he was now. *A useless wish*, he reminded himself.

"I started back on the mug shots." He carried his coffee to the table. "But we should order breakfast soon too."

"How did you get into the program?" Her amber eyes narrowed with suspicion. "Did you steal my password?"

"Steal is a harsh word," he said with a wry smile. "I—uh, have a good memory."

She shook her head with exasperation but joined him at the computer. She sipped her coffee, then gestured to the screen. "I know this is probably a useless effort, but I don't know what else we can do. Especially now that Rhy ordered me to stand down."

"I think that's best. I really don't want you to lose your job." He tapped on the mouse pad. "And you never know, we could stumble across something in here."

"Maybe." She didn't sound convinced as she reached for the room service menu. "Looks like they have typical breakfast choices. What would you like?"

"Eggs, toast, and bacon." He grinned. "I've been living on oatmeal since it's cheap and easy. Rosie's was the first meal out I've had in what seems like forever. I plan to enjoy this while I can."

That made her laugh. "I hear you. I eat a lot of mac and cheese for dinner too. But I warn you, the food here will not even be in the same stratosphere as Rosie's."

"Yeah, that was the best apple turnover ever," he agreed.

He was hyperaware of her sitting beside him as he went through more of the mug shots. Their arms brushed on occasion, and it took all his willpower not to wrap his arm around her shoulders, drawing her in for a hug.

"We don't have access to juvenile records, do we?" He continued scrolling through the photos. "I tend to pay more attention to the kids that come into the church, more so than the adults."

"Because you identify with them?" she asked, her head tilted to one side.

"Yes." He shrugged. "And because they're the ones who need the most help. Not that adults can't change their course, but it's the kids who are more vulnerable."

"Let me see if I can run a search based on age." She nudged the computer away from him to take over at the helm. "The best we can do is to look at those teenagers who were charged as adults."

He winced at that thought. Most likely, any teenager who was charged as an adult would still be in jail. Unless, of course, the charges were lowered as the result of a plea deal. But then he thought about the friends he'd once hung around with. Not Beau, he went to college, but there had been others. Maybe he would find some of them in there.

She worked the keyboard, then nodded. "Okay, here they are. More than I would have expected," she admitted.

He grimaced, knowing it was the never-ending cycle of poverty and violence. Yet his mother had worked hard as a housekeeper, and so had he, at least until she'd gotten sick. That was when he'd taken the wrong path, going for the easy money.

Yet that was the same path that had brought him to God.

A familiar face bloomed on the screen. He stared in shock for a moment, then turned to Raelyn. "This looks exactly like Tiger. Except maybe a couple of years older."

"Tiger?" She frowned, then nodded. "Oh yes, the kid with the orange Afro."

"Exactly." He was mixed race, too, and had used that similarity to get closer to Tiger. But the boy was skittish, sticking around long enough to eat but then had taken off. He looked at the name on the screen. Reggie Vallera. "I guess I didn't realize he had an older brother named Reggie."

"Or a cousin?" she asked.

"Maybe. Either way there is a really strong family resemblance." He continued staring at the screen. Had he seen Reggie at one point? Reggie had been arrested at the age of sixteen. Based on the date of his arrest being over five years ago, he felt certain Reggie was back out on the street by now.

And he wasn't a juvenile anymore.

A knock on the door indicated their breakfast had arrived. He jumped up, but Raelyn beat him to the door.

Cautious as always, she checked the peephole first, then opened the door. She handed him the tray, then tipped the server. "Thanks."

"You're welcome." The server quickly left.

The aroma of bacon and eggs made his mouth water. He pushed the computer aside, still trying to figure out when he may have seen Reggie Vallera.

Once they were seated, Raelyn surprised him by taking his hand. "I appreciate you saying grace," she said lightly.

"Always." His heart swelled with hope as he bowed his head. "Dear Lord Jesus, we thank You for this food we are blessed to eat. We ask for Your strength and guidance as we search for those who wish us harm. Amen."

"Amen," she echoed. "That was nice."

"Anytime." He took a bite of his bacon. "Mmm. Tastes as good as it smells."

"But still not as good as Rosie's." She laughed and nibbled on hers too.

They ate in companionable silence. He wished they could spend time together like this more often but knew that the moment the danger was over, she'd go back to her life, and he'd return to his church.

When they finished eating, he put their tray out in the hallway, then returned to the computer. He made a note of Reggie's name, before moving onto the next.

Raelyn was scrolling on her phone. "Did you know that Sergeant O'Malley was the same officer who arrested you and Donte Wicks?"

"Really?" He turned to face her. "I didn't recognize him."

"I'm not sure it's significant," she admitted. "I mean, he clearly works out of the third district. It makes sense that he'd be involved in arrests that took place there."

"I wonder why he didn't mention that last night." He thought back to those initial days in the hospital. All he remembered was the pain and being unable to move much because his ankle was cuffed to the bed. "I guess you're right, though. If O'Malley was there the night I was shot, he would have been the one to follow up on Donte Wicks."

"Yeah." She continued scrolling. "Donte was arrested about ten blocks from the church."

"Again, that's not surprising. Especially since it wasn't a church back then." He shrugged. "It was an old pizzeria that was renovated into a church over two years ago with help from Mayor Critten and the city councilmen."

She frowned. "Do you think someone hid something inside the church? Like before it was remodeled?"

"Maybe, but why would that matter now?" He didn't see what she was getting at. "I've been the church pastor for two years. Plenty of time for whoever hid something inside to come back and get it."

"Yeah, you're right." She sighed and set her phone down. "There's nothing else interesting on the arrest reports."

"I'm not finding anything else in these mug shots either." He went back to Reggie Vallera's photo.

Why were the kid's features so familiar? Because he'd been involved in the drug deal going down outside the church? More likely because of his resemblance to Tiger.

"Maybe you should ask an officer to go to Reggie's

address to see if Tiger is there." He didn't like turning on one of the kids, but Donte's murder changed things.

She nodded and reached for her phone, just as it rang. She winced and quickly answered. "Hey, Rhy, what's up?"

He wished she'd place the call on speaker so he could hear both sides of the conversation. But as it turned out, the interaction was brief. "Yes, we'll be there in ten minutes. Thanks."

"We're going to the precinct?" he guessed.

"Yes." Her smile was strained. "Sounds like Assistant Chief Michaels wants to chat."

He caught her hand in his. "Are you in trouble?"

"I don't think so." She was clearly downplaying the request from her boss. "Let's go. I don't want to be late."

He rose and followed her out of the hotel suite. They left the building the way they'd come in, through the side door. The Jeep was right where they'd left it.

They were on the road in less than a minute. Traffic was busy, though, especially around the courthouse. There were lots of pedestrians walking around, college kids from the university, he noticed. The same university the three girls he'd driven home a couple of nights ago also attended.

"You might have Grayson for a bodyguard moving forward—"

Her comment was cut short by gunfire. Their windshield shattered, and he could hear screaming from the students.

"Get down." Raelyn yanked him down so that their heads were below the dashboard. They were sitting ducks out here, and he feared the next burst of gunfire would find its mark.

Killing him once and for all.

CHAPTER TWELVE

Why did this keep happening?

Raelyn had stopped in the middle of the street when the windshield shattered and a car behind her slammed into the rear bumper of the Jeep. Not too hard, as they hadn't been going very fast. The driver laid on the horn, but she ignored it. She fumbled for her phone, even though she felt certain there were plenty of onlookers who were calling in the sound of gunfire. The morning commute was busy, tons of people around, which made it unusual that anyone would try to take them out here.

Unless the goal was to get them out of their vehicle and into the open?

"We're staying in the Jeep with our heads down," she told Isaiah as she pushed the 911 buttons on her phone. When the dispatcher answered, she gave the approximate location of their damaged vehicle. The dispatcher wanted her to stay on the line, but she disconnected, knowing they may not have a choice but to go on the move.

"The traffic will slow the response," Isaiah noted.

"But they're close too. Plenty of deputies near the courthouse." She knew the sheriff's deputies who are responsible for the security of the courthouse would not hesitate to respond to the gunfire. "We'll be safe."

"You think so?" Doubt laced his tone. "I'm not sure about that."

To be honest, she wasn't sure either. She tilted her head enough to meet his gaze. "God is watching over us."

He managed a smile. "True. I'll keep praying."

She nodded, listening intently. Then a deputy came up to bang on her driver's side window. She lifted her head enough to see the friendly face of Mike Callahan. "Mike?"

"Raelyn, unlock the door."

She hit the button on the handle, and he wrenched the door open. "Are you both okay?" His concerned gaze raked over her and Isaiah.

"I think so." She reached up to touch her cheek, belatedly realizing she was cut and bleeding. "Minor injuries don't count."

Mike nodded in agreement. He knew as well as she did that this situation could have been much worse. "Let's get you both out of here." He jerked his thumb. "My squad is only ten yards from here."

Looking past his shoulder, she could see his clearly marked sheriff's department vehicle. She slid out of her side as Mike ran around to Isaiah's passenger door. As a group, they lightly ran back to the squad. She felt a little guilty making Isaiah sit in the back caged-in area, but she was armed and needed to be up front in case the attacker tried again.

"I'll have to call for a tow truck for the Jeep," Mike said. "And get someone out here to direct traffic."

"I understand. The Jeep is an undercover vehicle for our precinct." She winced. "Which reminds me, I'm supposed to be having a meeting with the assistant chief in about fifteen minutes."

"Okay, you should probably let Rhy know you'll be late." Mike seemed to understand things were not going well. Of course, the gunfire that shattered the windshield was another big clue. "Let him know I'll get you down there as soon as I have additional backup."

"We need to get a first aid kit," Isaiah said. "Those cuts on Raelyn's face need tending."

"I'm fine." She wasn't worried about some shallow cuts. She turned in her seat to face him. "That bullet was meant for you, Isaiah."

Mike Callahan's eyebrow hiked up. "Oh yeah?"

"Mike, this is Pastor Isaiah Washington. He's been targeted by a gunman multiple times over the past few days." She made the quick introductions. "Isaiah, this is Deputy Mike Callahan. He's Rhy's cousin."

"Nice to meet you," Isaiah murmured. "Although I'm sorry it had to be like this."

"Me too. What church?" Mike looked interested, and she remembered the Callahans were believers like the Finnegans. Must be a family thing. Which would explain her lack of knowledge about God and Jesus. Her mother had never crossed a church threshold from what she remembered.

"The New Hope Church," Isaiah answered. "I'm sure you've never heard of it. It's relatively new and located on the north side."

"That's a rough area," Mike said with a nod. "Good for you opening a church there. I think I'll bring my wife, Shayla, and our two kids sometime."

Isaiah's eyes widened in concern. "Oh, that's not necessary. As you said, it's a rough area. I don't expect you to expose your family to danger."

"I'm sure it will be fine," Mike said, waving away his concern. "Although we'll need to figure out who has targeted you first."

"I couldn't agree more about the need to get to the bottom of these attacks." She scowled darkly. "I wasn't expecting this to happen. We spent the night at the City Central Hotel, and everything was fine, until this."

"Any idea how you were identified?" Mike asked.

"The Jeep," she answered without hesitation. The person who'd killed Donte Wicks must have seen their vehicle. Although how that same person had managed to track them here was a mystery. It was difficult to believe that anyone from the drug-running business had the ability to track a car through the DMV.

But there were other ways to do that. She abruptly straightened. "We need to check for a GPS tracker on the Jeep."

"I'll make sure we search for one," Mike assured her. "But you can't go out there now. Not while the gunman is still on the loose."

"Okay." She had to be satisfied with that. And who was the gunman anyway? Hugo Morrison had likely been the original assailant, but who had taken over for him? Was it Reggie, Tiger's brother? Or someone else?

Mike's radio crackled. She could see additional squads converging on the area. Mike glanced at her. "Sit tight. I'll be back in a minute."

She nodded, swallowing a knot of apprehension. She texted Rhy a brief message about the gunfire delaying their arrival, then scanned the area, noting there were at least a dozen cops milling about. The shooter would have to be crazy to try again.

But for all she knew, the guy was a little crazy. Or desperate. Or something.

"I'm sorry," Isaiah said softly. "I hate knowing you're putting your life and your career on the line for me."

She turned to look at him. "I put my life on the line for the public every day, so there's no reason to apologize. And I'm the one who broke the rules. I will take full responsibility for my actions."

"You're an amazing woman."

She tried not to blush. "I'm not. I'm just a cop." It seemed Isaiah wanted to see the best in her, but she knew she was far from perfect.

"You are," Isaiah repeated. "And God knows our sins and still cares for us."

That gave her pause. She hadn't really thought about it that way. But then Mike jogged back to the squad, opening the door and sliding in behind the wheel. "You were right, Raelyn. There was a GPS tracker on the Jeep. The lab is going to process it for prints."

"Thanks." She wanted to smack herself for being so careless. If Isaiah had been hit by one of those bullets, she would never have been able to forgive herself.

Mike pulled away from the curb, his cherry-red lights flashing to encourage cars to move over to give them room. Rhy had responded to her text, asking if anyone was hurt. She sent a quick response, assuring him they were fine and on their way with Mike Callahan.

As if being shot at wasn't stressful enough, she now had to face Assistant Chief Michaels. The guy scared her, and frankly, she'd rather be out on the street with nothing but her small backup weapon than have this meeting.

Not that she had a choice.

"This is all related to the initial shooting incident outside the church?" Mike asked.

"Yes." She glanced back at Isaiah for a moment, then added, "The first attempt on Isaiah was when he was standing outside his church. From there, the attacks have escalated to the point it's clear someone wants to kill him."

"I can't imagine who would have a grudge against a church pastor," Mike said with exasperation.

"I wasn't always a pastor," Isaiah said. "I was once a criminal too. But that was ten years ago. Our current theory is that the Chief, the guy in charge of the drug running in the city, has hired several people to come after me. Maybe because he thinks I know who he is, which I don't."

"I see." Mike frowned, then glanced at her. "You know we're here if you need us. Rhy's teammates are like family."

"I know, thanks." That wasn't as easy as Mike made it sound. Rhy was her boss, and the Finnegans and Callahans were family. Real family, by blood and DNA. Rhy was a great boss and cared about his team.

But going over Rhy to get help from his cousins sounded like a good way to get fired. If the assistant chief wasn't about to do that, already.

Mike pulled up in front of the precinct. She slid out and opened Isaiah's door. "Thanks, Mike. Will you keep me updated if prints are found on the GPS device?"

"Of course. You'll be the first to know." Mike lifted a hand. "Take care, Raelyn. Nice to meet you, Isaiah. Stay safe out there."

"We will." She shut the car door and led the way inside. Isaiah was unusually quiet behind her, sensing her anxiety. She had to admit Isaiah picked up on her moods far better than any man ever had.

Was that good or bad? She wasn't sure.

Rhy was waiting for them. He scowled when he saw her. "You said you weren't hurt."

"I'm not." Then she remembered the blood on her face. "It's not serious, do I have a minute to wash up?"

"Go ahead," Rhy agreed. "I'll let Michaels know you're here."

Her stomach knotted, but she made quick use of the time. She washed away the blood she'd accidentally smeared across her face. The cut wasn't deep, so she didn't think she'd need stitches.

She drew in a deep breath, trying to steady her nerves. Panic wouldn't help. She'd been in the army and a cop; this was all she knew. But there were likely other options out there. Security, right? She seemed to remember Trinity Medical Center hired security guards to patrol the campus.

For a moment, the thought of her burned home and the possible loss of her job nearly sent her to her knees. With an effort, she straightened her spine, schooled her features, and left the restroom. She followed Rhy to the assistant chief's office and knocked on the door.

"Come in," Michaels called.

Rhy offered a reassuring smile before turning away. Maybe it was intended to give her hope. She opened the door and stepped inside. She executed a quick salute, then stood at attention.

"At ease," Michaels said. "I heard about the fire at your home and these recent attacks. How are you holding up?"

"Fine, sir." She tried not to show her confusion. If he intended to kick her to the curb, he was taking the scenic route. "I have insurance to cover the fire, and I'm not hurt. The target of these attacks is Pastor Isaiah Washington.

Thankfully, he has not been injured either." *Yet*, she silently added.

Chief Michaels steepled his hands together. "I support and applaud your efforts to keep Washington safe. I wanted you to know that I've been contacted by Captain Sanchez of the third district. They're concerned you're running undercover operations in their district without keeping them informed."

So that's what this is about. That jerk Stern had gone up the chain of his command. She should have known. She gave a tight nod. "To be clear, I didn't execute an undercover operation in their district, but I did go there several times with Isa—er—Pastor Washington to find and interview suspects. These are people within his community and who are more likely to open up to him as he is one of their own. Unfortunately, those seemingly innocent attempts resulted in dire consequences. Including the recent murder of Donte Wicks, a former drug dealer in the area." She hesitated, then added, "I'm truly sorry that Captain Sanchez is upset. I did not intentionally leave them out of the loop."

"Captain Sanchez seems to think you should work with Officer Stern moving forward," Michaels said.

No! Her heart thudded painfully. That would be akin to working with a porcupine. "Sir, Officer Stern is taking the loss of his colleague Dillon Colbert, who was killed the night of the shooting, very hard. I'm not entirely sure he can be objective when it comes to this case."

"Yes, which is why I informed Captain Sanchez that we should bring a neutral party into the mix. After discussing this at length with Finnegan, I've asked for assistance from Officer Reed Carmichael out of the fifth district. That district butts up against the third, and they often share resources." Michael's eyes crinkled in a rare smile. "I know you and Reed will be able to work together on this."

"Me?" Her voice was a squeak. "Sir, I would love nothing more, but I'm on administrative leave . . ."

"Not anymore. Get suited up in your uniform. I know that you and Reed—with some input from Pastor Washington—will figure this thing out."

She felt her jaw drop but did her best not to show it. "Thank you, sir."

"Dismissed."

She didn't have to be told twice. She executed another crisp salute, then turned and left the office. After closing the door, she leaned against the wall for a moment to pull herself together.

Rhy had gone to bat for her. She knew full well Michaels leaned on Rhy when it came to operational issues.

This was what it felt like to have a real family. Even if they weren't connected by blood or DNA.

They were still family. And she was blessed to have them at her back.

ISAIAH SAT IN A CHAIR, his head bowed, and his hands clasped between his knees, praying that Raelyn would not lose her job because of him.

Please, Lord, she does so much good for the community, she doesn't deserve this.

"Isaiah?" He glanced up at Rhy's voice. "What's wrong?"

"I don't think it's fair for Raelyn to lose her job because she's helping me." He swallowed hard. "I'm the one that wanted to talk to Donte Wicks. He was my drug-dealer contact ten years ago, and I thought I could convince him to cooperate. This is my fault, not hers."

"Try not to worry, she's fine." Rhy clapped a hand on his shoulder. "I would warn her if the situation was that dire."

"You would?" He rose to his feet. "That's nice to hear."

Rhy flashed a smile. "I value every single member of my team. I would never hang one of them out to dry."

"I'm glad." He glanced over as Raelyn approached. She was smiling, too, and the heavy boulder of guilt rolled off his chest. "What happened?"

"The assistant chief seems to think we should partner with Reed Carmichael to continue working the case." She arched a brow at Rhy. "You could have warned me. I walked into that meeting expecting the worst."

"I would have, except you were running late, and Michaels has another meeting with the mayor's office very soon." Rhy glanced down at his watch, and added, "He's probably leaving now."

"Reed Carmichael?" The name sounded familiar, but Isaiah couldn't place it. "Do I know him?"

"He's a cop within the third district police station, they help cover the third district," Raelyn said with a wry smile. "You met him the day we were in my squad heading to your church when we were hit by gunfire, remember? He's Rhy's brother-in-law, too."

He nodded, remembering the incident.

"Figured I'd keep it in the family," Rhy joked. Then his gaze sobered. "I know the third district isn't happy with you, but working with Reed with approval from Sanchez will smooth things over. And this latest attempt against you and Isaiah took place outside both of those districts, which makes this a broader issue now for everyone within the police department. I'm glad you've been cleared to return to full duty. I'll issue you a replacement weapon until yours has been returned."

"Thanks, Rhy. I'm happy about this too. I need to change." Raelyn hurried toward the woman's locker room.

Isaiah didn't share her elation at being returned to full duty. Sure, he was relieved she still had her job, but he hadn't anticipated that she'd be heading back out into the line of fire.

"Hey, don't worry." Rhy must have sensed his dismay. "Raelyn is good at her job. And she'll have more support from Reed on this, which should help. The rest of our team is also available if needed."

"That is good news, thanks for that." He eyed Rhy curiously. "How many siblings do you have anyway?"

"Eight, and I'm the oldest of the group. We lost our parents eleven years ago yet managed to stick together as a family. The good news is that we're all happily married and living our best lives. We've also started the next generation of Finnegans." Rhy's grin lit up his face. "It's been amazing. Although, the path here wasn't an easy one. We've had our difficulties along the way, not unlike what you're experiencing now, but we have been truly blessed by God."

He didn't know of any large families that hadn't been broken up by divorce, death, or prison. For a moment, his mother's exhausted features flashed in his mind. She'd done her best; he was the one who'd failed her. "That sounds wonderful."

"It is. And you should know that we're here for you, Isaiah." Rhy's brown eyes were intense. "I know you're a man of faith. I admire your dedication to your church, especially within a difficult environment. We'll get this guy, whoever he is."

"Thank you." He did have faith in God and in Rhy's

team. Yet he couldn't relax, as his biggest concern was for Raelyn. He had hoped she'd be kept on administrative leave long enough for the third district to find this guy.

But as Rhy had mentioned, this was a broader issue now. No matter where he went, he would be targeted. Which made him think it would be better to find a spot to stay that was closer to his home and the church.

The church. Of course. Why hadn't he considered the possibility sooner? He was the one the Chief wanted. This was all about him and whatever the Chief thought he had done or would do at some point in the future.

What better way to put an end to this once and for all?

"You need to use me to draw this shooter into the open," he said as Raelyn walked up, dressed in her full uniform. "Set me up in the church and have cops hidden nearby to grab him before he can hurt anyone else."

"No way," Raelyn said. "We don't use civilians as bait for murderers."

"Hold on a minute, that might work," Rhy said thoughtfully.

"What?" Raelyn spun around to face him. "You never agree to putting innocent civilians in the line of fire."

"That's true, I normally wouldn't, but this is different. Isaiah is involved in this, likely from his past in dealing drugs. I think it's an idea worth investigating."

"Good. Because I am the one at risk here, regardless of whether you set me up in the church or hide me in some safe house." He turned to meet Raelyn's angry gaze. "If you would stop and think it through, you'd know I'm right. Look what happened mere blocks from the court-house? Think about how many innocent lives could have been taken if the shooter had missed us and struck a nearby pedestrian? Or another car? Maybe one with children inside? We must end this, Rae. The sooner the better."

A flash of pure agony darkened her expression, but then she tore her gaze from his to look at Rhy. "I'm on record as opposing this but obviously will follow through with whatever you decide."

Rhy nodded. "Thank you. I need to discuss the details with Joe. We won't do this without a good plan in place to keep everyone safe."

"Well, that's something," Raelyn muttered.

"Give me a few minutes. Help yourself to some of our really bad coffee." Rhy turned and walked away.

There was a long tense silence before Raelyn gestured to a small room off to the side of the main desk area. "This way."

He followed her into the tiny kitchenette. She poured two cups of coffee, handing him one before dropping into a chair. "This is a bad idea."

"I don't see an alternative." He took the seat next to her. The space was so small their knees bumped. "Raelyn, I worry about you getting hurt every moment you're protecting me. I know you're concerned about my safety too, but we'll never know who is responsible unless we do something drastic."

"Set you up to be killed?" She glared at him over the rim of her cup. "Yeah, I'd say that's drastic. And should be completely out of the question, no matter what Rhy and Joe say."

"What else can we do? Sit in another hotel and wait for something to happen?" He took a sip of the coffee that was at least three hours old, then set the cup aside. He reached for her hand, cupping it gently in his. "I need to get my life back and so do you. We've tried hiding out, and that hasn't exactly worked for us." He managed a smile. "Don't try to pretend you love sitting around watching me go through mug shots."

"I don't, that's true. But Hugo Morrison might tell us what we need to know," she insisted. "We could at least wait that long."

"And what if he doesn't cooperate?" He was pretty sure Hugo would rather go to jail than risk squealing on the Chief. Why else had he taken a shot at Raelyn when he could have surrendered? "Consider how Donte Wicks was killed to prevent him from talking. Don't you think Hugo knows what the Chief is capable of? There's no reason for him to work with us. Not if he values his own life."

She fell silent, staring down at their joined hands. Hopefully, she'd realize this was their best option.

Finally, she raised her gaze to meet his. "I don't want anything to happen to you, Isaiah."

His heart swelled with hope. He lifted her hand and kissed it. "I don't want anything to happen to you either, Raelyn. I care about you." He didn't add that if one of them had to die to put an end to this, he prayed that he would be the one to go.

Not her.

CHAPTER THIRTEEN

It was strange the way her hand looked so small in his. Raelyn was touched by Isaiah's concern for her.

"It will be fine," Isaiah said in a low voice. "Have faith."

Faith in God? Or in the team? Or both?

"Okay." She squeezed his hand, then stood. Deep down, she didn't like it. And was frankly surprised Rhy would even go along with Isaiah's plan to set him up at the church to draw the shooter out.

Glancing over to see Rhy and Joe with their heads together, she told herself they wouldn't be reckless. They wouldn't expose Isaiah to danger without a solid plan, but she still had a bad feeling about this. The church itself was in a rough neighborhood. And really, how many places would there be to hide members of the team anyway?

The basement could work. She wondered if Isaiah could convince the neighbors across the street to cooperate with them on this. They had given statements about the initial shooting, but that was a far cry from allowing a cop in their house or their yard.

She took a step toward her lieutenant and captain, but

Isaiah grasped her arm. She turned to face him. His blue eyes were intense. "Raelyn, you should know—"

"Rae? What's this about a plan?" Grayson interrupted whatever Isaiah was about to stay.

"Rhy and Joe are cooking it up." She didn't take her gaze off Isaiah. "What were you about to say? What do I need to know?"

"Never mind." Isaiah released her. "We can talk more later."

She frowned, assuming he'd wanted to mention something about the idea of setting himself up as bait to draw out the killer. She wished Grayson had held off for a few minutes, but now she turned to her teammate. "Did Rhy call you?"

"No, Joe sent a text." Grayson glanced to the side door where Steele and Jina had just come in. "I assume he included all of us, except Brock because he and Liana are on vacation."

Brock and Liana had renewed their wedding vows last month and were taking a well-deserved vacation that Brock referred to as their honeymoon. Apparently, they hadn't taken one when they'd originally gotten married a year ago, and Brock was determined not to make the same mistakes he had in the past.

She was happy for them; their love shone brightly during the ceremony. She'd also been a little sad over knowing she'd never have what they did.

Now, she wasn't so sure. Oddly, she couldn't imagine her life without Isaiah. Which was ridiculous since a relationship between them would never work out.

"Look, there's Roscoe and Zeke too." Grayson sighed loudly. "Roscoe, ditch the cowboy hat. You're not in Texas anymore."

"I'm still a Texan," Roscoe drawled. "Moving from one part of the country to another doesn't change that."

"Whatever, dude," Zeke said. "You look ridiculous."

"Where's Cassidy?" Raelyn joined the conversation to interrupt what she knew would be nonstop teasing.

"She's on her way," Jina said with a shrug. "She was on the other side of town when the text came through."

The three female officers tended to stick together in times where there was an excess of testosterone. Like now. She and Jina exchanged a knowing glance as the Zeke punched Roscoe in the shoulder.

"Hey, aren't you from the church?" Steele asked, looking at Isaiah. "You're the preacher, right?"

"Yes. Isaiah Washington." He nodded at the team that had gathered around them.

"You already met Grayson. The others are Steele, Jina, Roscoe, and Zeke," she said, gesturing to each one. "Cassidy is on her way, and I'm sure Flynn will arrive shortly. Brock is the only member of the team that is out of town."

"Yeah, he's missing the action," Zeke said with a snicker.

"Nice to meet you," Isaiah said, nodding to them. "I appreciate you coming to help us find and arrest the gunman."

"Just one gunman?" Roscoe asked with an arched brow. "From what I'm hearing, it seems like there's always another waiting in the wings."

"True," Raelyn agreed. "The attempts against Isaiah have continued to escalate since the initial shooting outside the church. We have Hugo Morrison in custody, but he's still in the hospital. He's in the ICU and on pain meds, so we can't interview him."

"And I don't think he'll cooperate, even if we can talk to

him," Isaiah added. "Hence this plan to draw the shooter out."

"What makes you think the next shooter will give up the boss?" Steele asked.

He had a point. She glanced at Isaiah, then shrugged. "I don't know," she admitted. "But it's worth a try."

Joe crossed over to join them. "We're still working out a few details. When the rest of the team gets here, we'll discuss the details in the big conference room." He turned to Isaiah. "Are you sure about this? If you want to back out, now is the time. We won't hold it against you or think any less of you. We will do everything possible to keep you safe, but there is no denying this plan comes with some risk."

"I'm sure." There was a steely determination in Isaiah's blue eyes. "I want the danger to be over. And that won't happen until we have the Chief in custody."

"No clue who the infamous Chief is, huh?" Jina wore a perplexed expression. "I'm kinda surprised he's been able to keep his real identity hidden for so long. Usually those kinds of secrets are not easy to keep."

"Yeah," Isaiah agreed with a frown. "Having grown up in that neighborhood, I can't help but think that I might recognize his legal name if I knew what it was."

"Well, that's the goal, right?" Raelyn tried to smile, thinking of how Donte Wicks was brutally murdered while they were outside in the Jeep mere feet from the property. "No one can stay anonymous forever."

Flynn and Cassidy arrived within five minutes of each other. She quickly introduced Isaiah before they headed into the large conference room. There wasn't enough room for everyone to sit, but they crowded around the table anyway. She sat beside Isaiah, while Joe stood at the front.

"Okay, we're still waiting to hear from Reed

Carmichael," Joe said. "He's stopping along the way to talk to the residents in the houses across the street from the church to see if he can use their place as a place to hide. We'll know more soon."

"What if they choose not to cooperate?" Isaiah asked.

"That's their right." Joe shrugged. "We'll make do."

Raelyn didn't love that idea and found herself praying the residents would allow the police to stay on their property. She almost reached for Isaiah's hand but managed to stop herself. Bad enough they were discussing a plan where he'd be used as bait. She did not want the team to know how deeply emotionally involved she was.

In the past few months, both Brock and Steele had faced difficult situations with women they cared deeply about. Emotion tended to interfere with the ability to think clearly and logically. She needed to stay focused on the mission before them.

"The idea is to get everyone in place during the night," Joe went on. "Then we'd like Raelyn to drop Isaiah off in front of the church early in the following morning. We assume someone is watching the church, waiting for him to show up."

She frowned, realizing this was going to take much longer than she'd thought. It was barely ten thirty in the morning. Full darkness was a good eleven hours away, and even then, they'd want to wait until after midnight to get into position.

"That seems like a long way off," Isaiah said, as if reading her thoughts. "We can't set this up sooner?"

"Not if they're watching the church," Joe said. "If they see cops getting into place, they'll sit back and wait us out."

"Isn't there another place we can use other than the church?" Jina asked.

"Unfortunately, Isaiah's house is a crime scene," she said. "I'm not sure it's been cleared by the third district officers after I shot Hugo Morrison there."

"And it needs to be cleaned up," Joe added. "The front door was repaired, but I'm sure there are blood stains inside."

"I can do that cleaning myself," Isaiah said. "My house would work as a secondary location. It wouldn't be unusual for me to head there to clean up after the shooting."

"We'll see what Reed Carmichael comes up with," Joe said. "We need to make sure we have at least two sniper locations for Jina and Steele."

"Hold on," Isaiah protested. "I thought the goal was to take the shooter alive, so that we can question him about the Chief?"

"That is the goal," Joe agreed. "But we'll have sharpshooters in place as a backup plan. We need to be prepared if things go south."

There was a long moment of silence as the team digested that. Isaiah still looked unhappy about that part of the plan, but she was relieved to know they had two excellent sharpshooters on their side.

"It's a last resort," Steele said reassuringly. "We don't want to shoot anyone when we head into these situations. But we do need to keep the community and you, safe."

Joe's phone rang. He pulled it from his pocket and said, "This is Reed. I'll be back in a few."

Those who were standing moved out of Joe's way as he left the conference room.

"Did anyone find Reggie?" Isaiah asked, breaking the silence.

"Who?" Grayson frowned.

"Reggie Vallera was convicted of selling drugs several

years ago. Isaiah identified him from a mug shot." She quickly explained about the possibility of Reggie Vallera being related to a teenager with the street name Tiger, because of his orange Afro.

"I think we should follow up on this Reggie lead," Steele said. "That's something we can do while we're waiting for nightfall."

"I planned on asking for a replacement vehicle so Isaiah and I could check out Reggie's last-known address." When Steele frowned, she added, "Its possible Reggie would open up to Isaiah over those of us in law enforcement."

"What happened to the Jeep?" Jina asked.

She was filling them in on the recent gunfire and the GPS device that Mike Callahan found on the vehicle when Joe returned.

"Okay, Reed was able to sweet talk one of the neighbors across the street to use their home." Joe grinned. "That's one less hurdle. We still need help to cover the back of the church. Which reminds me." Joe turned to Isaiah. "What was that building used for before it was renovated?"

"It was a pizza joint." Isaiah grinned. "Sometimes I can still smell the pepperoni."

"Great," Zeke muttered. "Now I want pizza for lunch."

"Me too," Flynn added. "But I want a pie with the works, not just pepperoni."

"We're discussing our upcoming mission, not lunch," Jina said sharply. "Stop talking about food already."

"I didn't see a large kitchen, though," Raelyn said, getting back to the church. "There was only a small kitchenette."

"The part of the church where the altar is located is where the original kitchen was," Isaiah explained. "The pews are set up where the restaurant tables were once located."

"Why did the pizza joint go under?" Cassidy asked. "You'd think people would love to have a pizza place so close."

"The owner was shot and killed one night when he was closing up," Isaiah said. "The shooters were looking for money, of course, but the owner resisted. He was shot and robbed. After that, his wife decided to move south."

Shot and killed? There was another long silence at that sobering news.

Beneath the edge of the table, Isaiah's hand sought hers. Her fingers interlaced with his, offering support.

She knew he faced danger on a regular basis, but the reality was like a sucker punch to the gut.

She desperately wished he'd move out of that neighborhood as soon as possible. Yet she also knew he never would.

"OKAY, that only reinforces the need to take the streets back from the drug dealers and other thugs," Joe said solemnly. "Getting the Chief off the street is a good place to start."

"I agree," Steele said. "I feel bad for those who have little choice but to live there."

"Mayor Critten is working on a strategy to decrease crime," Isaiah said. He released Raelyn's hand, knowing she wouldn't want the others to see their brief touch. "His son, Beau, was in my grade during high school. Beau was one of the few who made it out of the neighborhood to attend college." He didn't add that rumor had it Beau never finished his degree. But some higher education was better than none.

"I hate to say this, but based on recent events, I don't think Mayor Critten's strategy is working." Grayson spoke in a matter-of-fact tone. "I know change takes time, but the shoot-out in front of your church was not good."

"I know that." Isaiah was as frustrated as the rest of the neighborhood. "At least the mayor has added an additional twelve police officers to the third district."

The way the team members glanced at each other, Isaiah could tell they were not impressed. Remembering Officer Stern's attitude, he could understand why. Yet it was clear they needed to get the crime under control for those who wanted to live in peace to flourish. During the last two years he'd had his church, Isaiah had met enough good and decent people to know change was possible.

He prayed every day for the violence to end.

There was more discussion about how to cover the church without attracting undue attention. Flynn wanted to play the role of a homeless guy, and Joe agreed.

After they'd finished hashing out a few more details, Joe brought the meeting to a close. They'd done as much as they could for now.

Raelyn caught Joe before he could leave the conference room. "I need a vehicle, Joe. I'd like to swing by the last-known address of Reggie Vallera. I'm supposed to have Reed as a backup but he's not here yet and we don't have time to waste."

"Yes, I think I can convince him to talk to me," Isaiah said. "If not Reggie, then possibly his younger brother Tiger."

Joe frowned. "You're not heading back there alone. You need to take someone else from the team with you."

"I'll ride along," Grayson offered. "I was there when things went south with Hugo Morrison."

"Zeke and I can follow them," Jina said, joining the conversation. "We can hang back, though, only moving in if needed."

With four cops along for the ride, Isaiah wasn't sure he'd get anywhere with Reggie, but he felt as if he had to try. "Whatever you think is best."

"Fine." Joe glanced at his watch. "Rhy offered to buy pizza for lunch, so try to get back here by twelve thirty. This is a one-and-done scenario. Setting up the decoy operation is the priority."

"Understood," Raelyn said with a nod. "Thanks, Joe."

It took a few minutes to straighten out the vehicle situation. Joe offered Raelyn the use of his SUV since they didn't have many undercover cars available. Zeke had a spare sedan too, an older model that wouldn't look out of place.

He was feeling antsy by the time they were ready to go. Zeke and Jina left first so they could swing by for Zeke's sedan. He hoped they would stay out of sight while he, Raelyn, and Grayson approached Reggie's place.

He felt certain Reggie would see them coming from a mile away and take off. But he hoped Tiger was there. Having spoken to the younger boy at his after-service meals, he hoped he could convince him to help.

"We'll scope out the place first," Raelyn said. Grayson was driving while Raelyn gave him directions. "See if anyone is out and about."

"Okay." He doubted anyone from the neighborhood would be hanging around in plain sight, not after all the recent events that had taken place. The initial shooting, then the subsequent shooting of Hugo Morrison. Lastly the fatal shooting of Donte Wicks. Anyone involved would be hunkered down, waiting for the heat to die down.

"Reed was upset that we didn't wait for him," Grayson said. "I think he feels partially responsible for the area in his district."

"I'm just glad he got the neighbor to cooperate," Raelyn said. "That was huge. Did you tell him he could meet us here? I was given orders to include Reed in our investigation."

"I did. He's on his way," Grayson confirmed.

"What happens if I sit in the church for hours and no one comes after me?" Isaiah asked. "How long do we wait?"

Grayson and Raelyn exchanged a long look. "As long as it takes," Raelyn said. "It's possible things will stay quiet until dusk."

Yeah, that's exactly what he was afraid of. Long hours of waiting and watching would not work in their favor. He reminded himself that Raelyn and the others were well trained on this sort of thing.

Raelyn directed Grayson to drive by the dilapidated home that was supposedly Reggie Vallera's last-known address. Of course, there was no one sitting outside on the porch, the way there normally would be in the nicer weather months.

The entire block looked deserted, although he knew that wasn't likely. Many of these residents didn't work full-time jobs for a variety of reasons. Some legitimate, others not so much.

"Does Mayor Critten live around here?" Raelyn asked.

He barked out a laugh. "Not hardly. Why?"

"I was just wondering why he would come way out here to attend church services." She turned in her seat to look at him. "You said you went to school with his son, so he must have lived here at some point."

"He did, yes. But once he became mayor, he moved to a nicer area." He shrugged. "I can't blame him. That's what anyone would do if they had the chance."

"Yeah, I can see that." She shrugged, then added, "Do you know which house he lived in back then?"

"Yes, the one he rents to me," he said. "Mayor Critten still owns it. When he helped support the renovation of the church, he agreed to rent the house to me for a very reasonable rate. I jumped on the opportunity."

"That makes sense." She turned back to look through the windshield. "Hey, is that Tiger?"

He looked out the passenger window in time to see a young skinny kid with orange hair disappearing into a home across the street. It wasn't the place Reggie had listed as his address, but it was possible the guy had moved.

Or that the kids were hanging out there with someone else in residence.

"Do me a favor and go around the block," Raelyn instructed Grayson. "I don't think we want to park in plain sight."

"Agree," Grayson said. He turned right at the next intersection.

"Are you planning to approach that house rather than Reggie's address?" he asked. "That's a risk since we don't know how many are inside."

"This whole neighborhood is a risk." She waved an impatient hand. "We know Tiger went inside, and he knows you, Isaiah, so I think we should head there first." She glanced back at him. "Unless you'd rather stay behind."

"No, I'm going." He wanted Raelyn and Grayson to stay back but knew asking them to do so would be useless.

He swallowed hard as they parked the SUV and shut down the engine. Then he caught sight of an older model Ford rolling past them. "Is that Jina and Zeke?"

"Yes." There was no acknowledgment from either vehicle as the Ford turned at the next corner. "They're in position."

"Let's do this." He pushed open the door and climbed out. Both Raelyn and Grayson were dressed in uniform, so he didn't have high hopes for this encounter.

But he had to try.

They walked around the block in the opposite direction from where Jina and Zeke were staked out. He led the way along the eerily deserted side streets.

People were hiding indoors as if there was a plague sweeping through the neighborhood. As they passed one house, he caught the flutter of a curtain in front of the window.

And so it starts, he thought with a sigh. Phone calls would be made, warning others of the pastor and uniformed cops walking down the street.

No one would dare leave their homes now.

He rounded the corner and approached the house where he'd last seen Tiger. The place still looked deserted on the outside, but that was to be expected. He found himself quickening his pace to reach the front door.

He rapped on it hard, then called, "Tiger? It's Pastor Washington. We need to talk!"

No response. Which was really no surprise. He tried again.

"Tiger? Is Reggie with you?" He hammered his fist on the door. "Please open up. I just want to ask a few questions!"

Leaning forward, he listened intently but couldn't hear

anything from inside. He was reminded of how they'd done this at Donte's house, only to end up hearing gunfire.

"Hey! Stop! Police!" Raelyn's shout had him turning from the door. He caught the flash of orange movement as Tiger took off running from the back of the house.

Isaiah broke into a run, jumping down from the rickety porch to follow Tiger.

Behind him, he could hear Raelyn on the radio, letting Jina and Zeke know what was going on. He increased his pace, hoping to catch up with the boy, when he disappeared around the corner.

No! He couldn't let him get away!

Having a bit of a head start on Raelyn, he reached the corner first. He searched both sides of the street, intent on finding Tiger, but there was nothing.

Had the kid ducked into one of these houses? Or was he hiding somewhere?

"Where is he?" Raelyn asked as she and Grayson stopped beside him.

"I don't know." He walked down the street, still searching for Tiger.

"Nothing on this side," a female voice said through Grayson's radio.

"He couldn't have gone far," Raelyn groused. "He must be here."

The truth was that Tiger could have been anywhere. Some neighbors stuck together in an us-against-them stand against cops. Knocking on doors wouldn't help much.

"We can try Reggie's address," Grayson said, after another long five minutes of searching.

"Yeah, sure." Isaiah went along with the plan, waiting as Grayson fruitlessly knocked at the door. No one answered and this time, there was no movement either.

"Let's try the neighbors," Raelyn suggested. They split up to knock on more doors.

This wasn't going to work, Isaiah abruptly realized. No matter how well Joe and Rhy had planned to hide the officers nearby, the shooter wouldn't be fooled into attempting to kill him.

Not unless Isaiah was completely alone.

There was no other choice. He needed to ditch Raelyn and the rest of the tactical team.

From here on out, he'd work on his own.

CHAPTER FOURTEEN

Raelyn was frustrated by the lack of cooperation within the community. No one answered their doors, even though she could hear movement and in some instances televisions inside. No matter how many times she knocked or called out, there was no response.

It was because they were dressed in uniform, she knew. But they didn't really have a choice. Even if they had been wearing plain clothes, they'd have to identify themselves as MPD police officers and would meet the same resistance.

Yet they continued doing their best, going from door to door, hoping and praying one person would be brave enough to answer.

She wished they'd been able to catch up with Tiger. Or whatever the teenager's real name was. And where was Reggie Vallera? Still hiding inside the house listed on his last-known residence? Or had he gone elsewhere too?

After a full hour, they'd gotten nowhere. She returned to the corner of the street where Grayson, Jina, Steele, and now Reed, too, were standing. "Any luck?"

"Nope." Grayson glanced around. "Anyone else feel

like there are dozens of pairs of eyeballs boring into our backs?"

Steele chuckled. "Oh yeah. We're being watched big time."

"Always," Reed agreed.

Raelyn sighed. Then frowned. "Where is Isaiah?"

"He was going to houses, too, on the next street," Jina said. "I figured if anyone would have luck getting one of these residents to open their doors, it would be him."

"Yeah, but he's also been targeted by gunfire more times than I can count." She mentally kicked herself for not keeping an eye on him. "Let's go pick him up. We're wasting our time here."

"Fine with me," Grayson said. "I wish we could have spoken to either Reggie or Tiger, though. We could use a little intel before we kick off the main event later tonight."

Raelyn still wasn't fond of that idea but had resigned herself to the inevitable. "I just hope the neighbor Reed talked into cooperating with us doesn't change her mind."

"She won't," Reed assured her. "She likes me." They turned and headed up to the next corner. Going around the block, she searched for Isaiah.

"Are you sure this is the block?" she asked Jina. "Maybe he turned right to head west rather than turning left to head east."

"That's what he said." Jina frowned. "Maybe we should split up and cover both blocks, just in case."

"I'll stick with Raelyn," Grayson offered. "Jina, you and Steele should head to the west. Reed, take the north."

With a nod, the two officers turned away. Raelyn glanced at Grayson. "I'm worried about Isaiah. What if someone invited him in and killed him?"

"We'd have heard the gunfire," Grayson said. "Besides,

he knows these residents better than we do. I'm sure he'll be fine."

"Yeah. Okay." She tried to smile, but her stomach knotted with tension. She was upset that Isaiah had gone off on his own without telling her.

They'd been working well as a team. Or so she'd thought.

She and Grayson strolled along the sidewalk, staying on opposite sides of the street. She searched homes for an indication that Isaiah was inside one of them talking with the owner or renter.

By the time they had reached the end of the block, the knot in her stomach was tighter than a drum. Something was wrong. Even if Isaiah was inside, it wasn't likely the conversation would take this long.

She lifted her hand to the radio. "Jina? Do you and Steele have anything?"

"Negative," Jina replied.

"Reed?" she asked.

"Negative," he repeated.

"I don't like this, Grayson." She joined her teammate on the other sidewalk. "He's in trouble."

"Maybe he headed back to the car?" Grayson sounded calm but looked just as concerned as she was.

"Let's go." She turned and jogged to the street where they'd left Rhy's SUV. Thankfully, it was still there and appeared undamaged. Maybe the area residents had instinctively known it was a cop car and stayed away.

But it was also empty. Isaiah wasn't sitting there, waiting for them.

She called the disposable phone she'd gotten him. It rang and rang, but there was no answer. Not even a voice mailbox.

"I made him ditch his phone," she said, turning anguished eyes toward Grayson. "I felt certain he'd been tracked by the device. He's not answering the cheap one we replaced it with, and I'm not sure we can track it either."

"Hey, it's okay, we'll find him." Grayson seemed to know she was on the edge. "He couldn't have gone too far on foot."

"Yeah. I guess." That wasn't exactly reassuring. She reached for her radio. "We're taking the SUV to search for him. You guys may want to use the sedan too."

"Roger that," Jina agreed. "Stay in touch."

"Ditto," Reed added.

"We will." She wished she'd given Isaiah a radio. A better phone. Anything that would make it easier to find him.

If Isaiah had already been attacked and was lying dead in one of these homes or back alleys, she'd never forgive herself.

Grayson didn't object when she slid in behind the wheel of the SUV. Over the past few days, she'd gotten to know the neighborhood better than he did.

But not nearly as well as Isaiah. And that thought gave her pause.

"He left on purpose," she said, half to herself.

"You think so?" Grayson asked.

"It's the only thing that makes sense." She smacked her palm on the edge of the steering wheel. "He left to draw out the assailant on his own."

Grayson whistled. "Brave move."

"And stupid since we had a plan to set him up in the church anyway." She turned at the next corner. "We'll check the church first. That must be where he is."

"Unless the Chief snatched him off the street," Grayson

said. When she scowled, he added, "Come on, Rae. We need to consider all possibilities."

He was right. This wasn't the time to make assumptions. "Call Rhy. Let him know Isaiah is MIA. See what he thinks."

As Grayson used his phone to make the call, she drove to the church. But when she went to park in front of the building, Grayson shook his head and waved his hand, indicating she should keep going.

She drove through several additional streets before pulling over to the curb. Grayson was still listening to whatever Rhy was saying.

"Yeah, okay. We're roughly three blocks from the church. I'll let Jina, Steele, and Reed know they should stay back too." He pocketed his phone. "Rhy's not happy with the change in plan."

"We didn't make the change," she protested. "Isaiah did."

"I know that." Grayson sighed. "Rhy is going to talk this through with Joe. We may escalate the time frame of the original plan."

"How are we going to remain hidden in daylight?" She tried not to sound as annoyed as she felt.

"I think that's the biggest hurdle," Grayson agreed. "But we can get Flynn in place as a street bum. And he's going to tell Reed to sneak into the neighbor's house across the street."

"What are we supposed to do? Sit and wait?" When he shrugged and nodded, she clenched her teeth and looked away.

What had possessed Isaiah to take off like that? Especially knowing there was no one stationed nearby to intervene on his behalf?

Why, Lord? She closed her eyes for a moment, struggling to maintain her composure.

"Don't worry. Isaiah's tough." Grayson awkwardly patted her arm. "He'll be fine."

"You weren't there when he was targeted by gunfire." She appreciated his attempt to make her feel better, but she had been a part of this from the beginning. The initial attempt to shoot him when she'd been about to arrest him.

It seemed like eons ago now. So much had happened since then.

Like their incredible kiss.

No, she couldn't go there. Not now. *Think.* She needed to think! "I need to get out of this uniform." She searched her memory. "There's a used clothing resale shop a mile from here."

"Rhy said to wait . . ."

"The original plan isn't going to work," she interrupted. "I need a change of clothes. Let's go already. I'll change during the time it will take Rhy to get back in touch with us."

"Fine." Grayson threw up his hands in frustration. "But don't say I didn't warn you."

"Yeah. I know." She told herself that changing out of her uniform wasn't going against Rhy's orders. But depending on how things played out from this moment on, she very well may get herself in trouble.

The trip to the used clothing store didn't take long. But finding clothes that fit did. She finally settled on a pair of jeans that had paint splatters on them and a long-sleeved T-shirt that had badly faded in the wash. She found a black belt that fit if she used the last notch, along with a baseball cap to cover her hair. Armed with her new items, she directed Grayson to stop at the nearest gas station so she could change.

The one concession she made was to take the holster from her utility belt and to slip it on the new one. The long-sleeved T-shirt was baggy enough that the gun wasn't too obvious.

She eyed herself in the mirror knowing the disguise—such as it was—would have to do.

"I'm not sure this is a good idea," Grayson muttered when she joined him in the SUV.

She was pretty sure it wasn't. But that was okay. She didn't care.

She would risk her job and more to save Isaiah's life.

ISAIAH RECOGNIZED the number on his disposable phone as Raelyn's. Shame and regret washed over him as he pressed the end call button without answering.

He'd made his decision. Good or bad, he'd deal with whatever came.

Sitting in his tiny office in the church made him think of that initial shooting, the one in which he'd made the anonymous call to the police about a drug deal going down. The call that had started the train speeding forward until it had crashed into the wall in a giant wreck.

It was fitting that he was here now, hopefully bringing this to an end. He didn't want to die. Didn't want to leave Raelyn without letting her know how much he loved her, but this was the best solution for all of them.

Having officers sit outside the church for hours on end while nothing happened would be useless. He'd made sure that he was alone when he'd walked up to the front of the church and unlocked the door. He'd even glanced behind him, scanning the street as he stepped inside. It hadn't been as difficult as he'd thought to make himself a target.

Of course, no one had come to find him yet. And he wasn't sure the Chief would send anyone until it was later in the day. The problem with spring was daylight saving time. It wouldn't get dark outside until eight thirty or nine o'clock at night.

That was a long time to sit here, waiting for the trap to spring. And he wasn't armed with anything but a small paring knife that he'd found in the kitchenette. It was sharp, but no match against a gun.

He stared at his notes, scribbled ideas for what he would preach about on Sunday. At this point, even with offering a free meal, he doubted anyone would bother to attend church. The violence outside would keep those few law-abiding citizens away. And the possibility of the police showing up would keep the rest away.

For the first time, it occurred to him that he might not have a congregation anymore. Even with the mayor's support, he couldn't force people to attend services. Much less listen to what he had to say.

How could he instill the word of God and hope into the community if no one came to hear His word? A wave of helplessness hit hard.

He'd failed in the Lord's mission.

Holding his head in his hands, he struggled to maintain his composure. It wasn't as if he hadn't failed before.

But this one hurt deep down in his soul.

He'd thought God had spared his life for a reason. So far, it didn't seem as if he'd done anything worthy of being saved.

After a long moment, he managed to pull himself

together. Maybe it wasn't a lost cause. If he could entice the Chief to make another attempt to kill him, and the police found and arrested him, the neighborhood would be viewed as a safer place to be.

Wouldn't it?

He froze when he heard the sound of a shoe squeaking on linoleum. Someone was in the kitchenette.

This was it. Grabbing the small paring knife, he palmed it, hoping the intruder wouldn't notice until he was close enough to use it. Then he stood and moved around the desk, edging out of the office as quietly as possible.

A drawer in the kitchenette opened, and he heard rummaging sounds. What in the world? Then he heard the crinkle of plastic.

Crackers. He kept crackers in the drawer for the soup he provided in the after-service meal.

He continued easing along the wall until he could see into the kitchenette. And he wasn't surprised to find Pinky standing there, munching on a packet of saltines as if he hadn't eaten in hours. Maybe days.

Isaiah's heart squeezed in his chest. "Hello, Pinky. I have more food if you're hungry."

The kid spun like a top, nearly falling over in his haste. Cracker crumbs clung to the corner of his mouth and dusted his shirt.

"Hey, it's okay. You're safe here." Isaiah offered his most reassuring smile. "You're not in trouble. I'm alone. There's no one else with me."

"Where's the girl piggy?" Pinky asked, trying to sound tough, despite the cracker crumbs. To Isaiah's eyes, he looked uncertain and defeated.

"I ditched her." He slid the paring knife into his pocket. "There's water in the fridge and some lunch meat. We can make sandwiches. And I think there's canned soup in the cupboard, I'll heat that too." He wished he had more to offer the boy. "Have a seat and I'll get you something to eat."

Pinky looked suspicious, poised as if to run. But then his shoulders slumped, and he dropped into the closest chair.

Isaiah took a moment to rummage in the fridge. He pulled out the small amount of ham that had been left behind and made a quick sandwich. The bread wasn't fresh, but it wasn't moldy either. He doubted Pinky would care. Then he opened two cans of beef vegetable soup, poured the contents into bowls, and set them in the microwave on high.

Pinky wolfed down the sandwich in two minutes. Then he swiped his hand over his mouth, and muttered, "Thanks."

"You're welcome." He sat down next to the boy. "You're not in any trouble," he repeated.

"Yeah, sure." Pinky snorted. "That's why I been forced to hide like a rat these past few days."

"I'm sorry about that." He tried to catch the teen's gaze, but Pinky looked everywhere except at him. "Thank you for leaving the Glock."

That made Pinky glare at him. "I didn't do nuthin'."

"Okay, but I'm still grateful to have the gun." He tried to think of a way to get the boy to talk. "I'm sorry you've had to hide out."

Pinky lifted a shoulder. "Better than facing my old man."

Every time Isaiah thought about how his father had slammed his pinky finger with a hammer, it made his blood boil. But anger wouldn't help now. He needed answers. "The Glock was wiped clean, no fingerprints. And it was used to kill Officer Dillon Colbert."

Pinky looked away, hunched his shoulders even more, and played with his water bottle. "So?"

"I know you didn't shoot him," Isaiah said. "I know someone else killed that cop, then forced you to take the gun."

Pinky's brown eyes widened in surprise. "Did you see us?"

He hadn't known for sure until Pinky's reaction confirmed it. He knew how things worked on the street. Older teens often pulled younger ones into the life of crime, knowing that the DA's office sometimes treated them with more leniency.

But not when it came to killing a cop. That was like a death sentence. If Pinky had been found with the gun, he would have been tried as an adult and sentenced to life in prison without the chance for parole.

And that made him all the more ticked off over how this had all gone down. He wanted the person responsible to pay for this crime.

"Talk to me, Pinky," he urged. "I promise I can help smooth things over with the police if you tell me what really happened."

"Whose gonna believe me?" Pinky scowled and shook his head. "Not those pigs. They'll toss me in jail and leave me there to rot." The kid's lower lip trembled. "My ole man isn't going to help me by getting a lawyer, that's for sure. Everyone knows those freebies are useless. They don't care if we go to jail or not."

"Who shot the police officer?" He leaned forward, his gaze holding the boy's. "Please, Pinky. I promise I can help you. Just be honest with me and I'll make sure you're treated fairly."

There was a long silence. So long that he felt certain

Pinky wouldn't say. Then finally the kid opened up. "It was Reggie. His brother Tiger made me take the gun." Pinky's voice was full of defeat. "But they'll both deny it. And that's why it doesn't matter. It's my word against theirs. Two against one. And I'm nobody."

"You're not nobody; I believe you. And I care about you too." Isaiah hadn't realized Reggie had been out there, but it explained a lot. Especially how Pinky ended up with the Glock. Before he could say anything more, though, the microwave dinged.

He stood to remove the soup, intending to stir it when he heard another sound. That's when he realized he'd made his second biggest mistake. Not checking the back door to make sure it was locked after Pinky had found his way inside.

They were trapped.

"Well, well," a voice said. "Nice to have both of you in one place."

He turned from the microwave and took a step to the side so that his body was in front of Pinky's. Then his jaw dropped in shock when he recognized the familiar face of Beau Critten. His former classmate.

The mayor's son.

Somehow, he managed to face Beau with a calm expression despite the thundering of his heart against his ribs. "Hey, Beau. I haven't seen you in ages. What brings you here to the New Hope Church? I don't remember you attending services with your father recently."

"Don't give me that church bull," Beau sneered. That was when Isaiah noticed Beau held a gun in his hand.

Isaiah slipped his hand into his pocket and closed his fingers around the small paring knife. He felt better having a weapon, even though he wasn't at all sure he'd have the chance to use it.

"I'm sorry, I thought—"

"I don't give a rip if you're Daddy's pet project," Beau said, talking over him. "You've been a thorn in my side long enough. I knew it was a matter of time before you ratted me out. I'm here to eliminate the problem, once and for all."

"The problem? How am I a problem for you? My mission is one of peace, nothing more. And I feed the members of the community after each service," he added, striving to get through to the young man standing before him. "How is that a threat to you?" He needed to keep Beau talking in case Raelyn, Grayson, and the others were someplace nearby.

He never should have sneaked off without telling them. Especially Raelyn. As he faced certain death, his heart ached for what he might never have. He should have told her how much he loved her.

Yet as he faced Beau and his gun, Isaiah's biggest concern was the young boy behind him. He had no doubt that killing Pinky was part of Beau's plan to get rid of the problem. And why not? Pinky was the last person to have the Glock that killed Officer Colbert. Raelyn had seen that for herself.

With Pinky dead, it would be easy to place the blame on him. And the other kids, like Reggie and Tiger would adamantly insist Pinky had done it.

He still had his hand on the knife and wished he'd learned how to throw one. But he didn't. He was afraid Beau would shoot him in the chest before he could get his arm back for the attempt.

"You're a rat," Beau hissed, as if desperate to get everything off his chest too. "I know you spilled your guts about

Donte Wicks while you were in the hospital. And it was only a matter of time before you told the police about me too."

Me too? As in—

"Wait. You're the Chief? All this time you've been running the drug dealing in this neighborhood?"

Beau let out a harsh, humorless laugh. "Yes, I'm the brains behind the entire operation. Daddy thinks I have a nice legit job. And I do. Just not the stupid office job he helped me get. Oh, I do show up from time to time, but I don't stick around all day." He grinned. "They won't fire me because I'm the mayor's son. My one year of college is all it took for people to see me differently. But I'm smarter than they ever knew."

The news rocked him back on his heels. He'd never once expected the mayor's son to be the one in charge. Especially not for the past ten years! Longer than that, really, as he knew the Chief was in charge for at least two years before Isaiah got sucked into the life. At least, that's what Donte had told him.

All this time, Beau was running things. And Isaiah had never known the truth. He felt like an idiot.

"Well, that explains a lot," he said finally. "But you're wrong about me ratting you out, Beau. I had no idea that you were the Chief. Donte never told me. Neither did Hugo. Honestly, I'm impressed you were able to keep your identity a secret for so long."

"Yeah. And it's going to stay that way." Beau lifted the gun. "You know that old saying—if you want the job done right, do it yourself? Well, this is me, taking care of getting rid of you and that idiot Pinky once and for all."

This is it, he thought. Then he caught a glimpse of a

shadow moving behind Beau. Raelyn? Or one of the others? There wasn't a moment to waste.

"Gun!" he shouted. Then turned and threw himself over Pinky, protecting the teen as much as he could as the sharp report of gunfire reverberated through the room.

CHAPTER FIFTEEN

When Isaiah yelled gun, Raelyn fired at the man standing with his back to her. She was close enough that she took a chance and aimed for his thigh, which made him scream in pain and fall to the floor.

She rushed forward just as Beau Critten brought his gun around toward her, his face a mask of pain and fury. She instinctively ducked.

"No!" Isaiah lunged forward, his right hand crashing down on Beau's arm.

Beau screamed again and dropped the gun. "You stabbed me!"

He had? She couldn't see much as whatever Isaiah had used was buried deep in the muscle of Beau's bicep.

"Beau Critten, you're under arrest for murder. You have the right to remain silent; anything you say can and will be used against you in a court of law." She continued reciting the Miranda warning as she slapped handcuffs around the man's wrists. Then she used her phone to let Grayson know she had the situation under control.

"You shot me!" Beau spewed curses at her. "I'll have

your badge for this! Do you know who I am? I'm the mayor's son! You'll never work as a cop again!"

She ignored Beau's theatrics, turning her attention to Isaiah and Pinky. She hadn't known Pinky was in the room, but that explained why Isaiah had turned away after warning her about the gun.

"Are you okay? Anyone hurt?" she asked.

"Raelyn." Isaiah pulled her into his arms for a tight hug. "I knew you'd come. I knew if I kept him talking long enough, you would come."

She wanted to point out that he shouldn't have left in the first place but snaked her arms around his waist and hugged him back, burying her face against his chest. She'd been afraid Beau had gotten a shot off, and at such a close distance, she knew he wouldn't have missed.

"I almost lost you," she whispered.

"I know. I'm sorry." He kissed her temple. "I love you."

Love? She lifted her head in shock, but of course, that's when Grayson, Steele, Reed, and Jina barged into the room. With a sigh, she pulled out of Isaiah's embrace. But she couldn't go far, the small kitchenette wasn't big enough for all of them.

"He needs a bus." Raelyn gestured to her cuffed perp. "I audio recorded the conversation where he alluded to killing Donte Wicks and admitted he was in charge of the drug dealing. And I'm sure there will be other charges once we fully investigate him."

"He's the Chief. The man coordinating the drug dealing here for the past ten to twelve years," Isaiah said. "He thought I knew his identity, so he threatened to kill me and Pinky."

She turned to see Pinky cowering in the corner of the room. He looked scared to death, not at all like the kid with the false bravado when he'd held Isaiah at gunpoint that first day.

"Pinky. Are you hurt?" She cautiously approached, as if he were a cornered wild animal.

The boy shook his head. Then his gaze darted to Isaiah. "He saved me."

She smiled and nodded. "I know. Isaiah is a brave man. He believed in you all along, Pinky. He never once thought you shot that cop."

"I didn't," Pinky insisted. "It was Reggie."

She had heard and recorded most of what had been said. She couldn't wait to hand it all over to the DA's office. "I believe you. It's okay. I'm not going to arrest you."

Pinky gave a jerky nod, edging slightly closer to Isaiah. She decided it was better not to push. The poor kid had just been threatened at gunpoint by a man who had ruthlessly ran the streets.

But no more. She didn't care who his father was. Raelyn intended to make it her mission to make sure Beau Critten spent the rest of his life behind bars.

"What's in this guy's arm?" Grayson asked, kneeling beside the injured Beau.

"Paring knife," Isaiah answered. "I stabbed him to keep him from shooting Raelyn."

"Nice job," Grayson said with frank approval.

"Good one," Reed agreed.

"I'll sue you all," Beau screamed with frustration.

"You have the right to remain silent, and I suggest you use it," Steele said mildly. "We've been recording this from the moment Raelyn came into the church."

She had to smile when Beau's jaw dropped in shocked surprise and the color leeched from his face. She could tell he was trying to remember everything he'd said, but then he let out a piteous moan and closed his eyes.

The third district police officers arrived on the scene along with the EMTs. She ushered Isaiah and Pinky into the main area of the church to give the EMTs room to work over Beau Critten.

Reed, Steele, Jina, and Grayson joined them. "This is nice," Steele said with a smile. "Small, but quaint."

"Yeah, but I smell pizza," Jina complained.

That made the entire group burst into laughter, except for Pinky who looked confused.

The kid turned to Isaiah. "You said you only had soup and sandwiches."

"They're talking about this place, the church." Isaiah waved a hand toward the altar. "This building used to be a pizzeria."

"I love pizza," Pinky said with a sigh.

"We'll get you some as soon as we can," Isaiah promised. He glanced at Raelyn who shrugged.

"Sure, why not?" She could go for some pizza herself. "Although I need to talk to your parents, Pinky. They need to know what happened here. And that you're not a suspect anymore."

"There's just my dad." Pinky hunched his shoulders. "Mom ran away six months ago."

Really? Raelyn glanced at Isaiah who appeared surprised by the news too. "Well, I still need to speak to your dad," she said.

Pinky grimaced and looked away, clearly not happy. She had a bad feeling that a cop showing up on Pinky's father's doorstep would only cause trouble for the boy. The thought made her angry, as if hearing his son had almost been shot would cause Pinky's father to act out.

The image of Pinky's father slamming a hammer on his son's hand would not leave her alone.

Oh yeah, she wanted to face off with him all right. Yet it might be smart to take someone from the department of health and human services with her.

And Isaiah too.

"I'll come with you," Isaiah said, reading her mind. Or maybe he was trying to console the skinny teenager. "I'll make sure you don't get in trouble over this."

"Whatever," Pinky muttered. He clearly had no faith in the system.

"You again," a snide voice said from the hallway. She turned to see Officer Stern standing there. "Let me guess. You weren't satisfied with shooting Morrison, so you also shot the mayor's son."

"Yep." She crossed over to hand him her weapon for the second time in as many days. "He threatened to kill Pastor Washington and this teenager. Oh, and don't worry, this time I have an audio recording of the entire interaction."

"Oh yeah?" Stern's voice held doubt. She could feel Grayson, Reed, Jina, and Steele coming up to stand around her for support.

"Yes. You'll be glad to know that Pinky has identified Reggie Vallera as the person who killed your friend." Her tone softened. "I'm really sorry for your loss, Stern. None of us want to lose a brother or sister in blue."

"Reggie Vallera?" Stern looked dazed at the news. "Are you sure?"

"Yes. Reggie's younger brother, a kid who goes by the street name of Tiger, was there too. I'm sure we can convince him to cooperate." Once they found him. But that was up to the third district officers now.

They had the Chief in custody. The news of Beau's

arrest would spread throughout the community like wild-fire. Sure, one of Beau's underlings would try to step up to take over, but she hoped that Beau was cowardly enough to spill his guts for the chance of a lighter sentence once he realized they had him cold and that he was out of options.

The mayor's son didn't strike her as the type to do well in prison.

"Thanks." Stern offered a chagrined smile. "I'm sorry I've been a jerk. I owe you for helping to bring the Chief down."

"No, that's not true. We're all in this together." She remembered how upset the tactical team had been when they'd lost Kyle last Christmas. Time for her to cut Stern some slack.

More officers arrived, and the scene was chaotic for the next hour or so as statements were given and evidence was collected. The phone recording she'd done had been sent to both Rhy and Captain Sanchez. As soon as they were able to leave the area, she took Isaiah and Leon Smith, a.k.a. Pinky, to the closest pizza place.

Pinky ate as if he were starving, and she told him twice to slow down. "You can take the leftovers home," she told him. "Cold pizza isn't too bad."

Leon stared down at his plate for a long moment. "I would rather you stay away from my dad. He won't like you bringing me home."

She exchanged a concerned look with Isaiah. "Leon, has your dad hurt you again?"

The boy lifted a shoulder. "I dunno."

That was a yes in her book. Her house was burned to a shell, but they could clean up Isaiah's place and stay there for a while. She glanced at Isaiah, who obviously knew what she was thinking and nodded.

"We'll head to my place for a bit." Isaiah rested his hand on Leon's shoulder. "You'll stay with me until we can talk to your father."

"Really?" Leon looked up at him with suspicion. "How come?"

"Because I want you to be safe," Isaiah said. "Raelyn does too. But we'll need to do some cleaning at my place, and I expect you to help."

The boy, who suddenly looked much younger than his fifteen years, nodded, his gaze bright. "Okay. I can help clean. Thank you."

Her heart squeezed for him, and she knew without being told that Isaiah would find a way to be registered as a foster home for the boy. She admired Isaiah more than she could say and wondered again what he'd meant when he said he loved her.

Like as a friend? Friends could love each other, right? She pretty much loved her teammates, but that didn't mean she wanted to date any of the single guys.

Eww. Even the thought of that made her wince. They were more like brothers to her. Jina and Cassidy were the sisters she'd never had. Jina would help her out in a heartbeat, but the team sharpshooter didn't allow anyone to get too close.

She'd always assumed Jina had a similar background to hers. When you were a kid betrayed by adults, it wasn't easy to let your guard down.

Yet here was Leon, doing that despite what he'd been through.

With the leftover pizza boxed up, they left the restaurant and headed to Isaiah's house. To her surprise, there was a man standing on the front porch, swaying a bit as he swigged from a bottle.

"My dad," Leon whispered. "We shouldn't go there."

"What's his name?" she asked in a low tone.

"Eddie. But he's mean. You don't want to go there," Leon said, hanging back.

"Stay with Isaiah, okay?" She had her badge but not her gun. She hoped she wouldn't need it.

"Rae," Isaiah protested, but she ignored him.

"Mr. Smith? Eddie Smith?" She didn't smile as she mounted the stairs to meet him on the porch. "I'm police officer Raelyn Lewis."

"You that piggy looking to jam up my boy?" Smith sneered. He took another swig from the bottle of whiskey, although she could tell he was already intoxicated. His eyes were red, and he couldn't seem to stand straight. His face was drawn into a mask of anger. He reeked as if he'd been on a three-day bender, and maybe he had.

"Leon isn't in any trouble." She tried to hold his gaze. "But you are. Unfortunately, Eddie, you are trespassing on private property. I suggest you leave."

"It's a free country," he spat, clearly not understanding what he was saying.

"That doesn't give you the right to trespass. This house belongs to Mayor Critten who rents it to Pastor Washington. Now, I'm asking you again. Please leave."

"I tol' Leon to stay away from the preacher." Mr. Smith slurred his words, but the glitter of anger in his eyes indicated he was still a threat, drunk or not. "Don't want nuthin' to do with that church."

"Eddie, when is the last time you've seen your son?" she asked. "Before today. When did you last make him breakfast, lunch, or dinner?"

"I dunno. Who cares?"

"I do." She stepped closer, trying not to gag at the

stench. "I plan to call child protective services, Eddie, because I don't believe Leon is safe in your care. I think you've been neglecting him and your duty as a parent."

"Pig!" he screamed and lashed out with the bottle, aiming for her head. She ducked, then spun and kicked out with her foot, jamming the heel of her foot into his groin. He crumpled like a rag doll, screaming in pain.

"Eddie Smith, you're under arrest for assaulting a police officer." She had used her cuffs on Beau but still had a couple of plastic zip ties. "You have the right to remain silent, so I suggest you do that." She would have recited the rest of his rights, but Eddie was moaning and holding his crotch, and she doubted he was in any condition to hear them.

She bound his wrists, then stepped back to call a squad. She knew there were likely several police officers still at the New Hope Church.

Stern arrived less than two minutes later. "Are you some kind of magnet for trouble, or what?"

"Hey, I didn't plan this, he was here when we got here. He tried to assault me, and he was trespassing on private property." She scowled. "I don't think he's fit to be a parent, and I'd like him booked for assault, battery, and drunk and disorderly too."

"Yeah, yeah. I might owe you, Lewis, but he better not puke in my car," Stern said with a sigh. "Come on, Eddie. Time for another stint in the jail."

"Another stint?" she echoed.

"Oh, he's been arrested several times," Stern informed her. "But assaulting a police officer might be enough to keep him locked up for a while this time."

She hoped it did, but she knew the system was overcrowded with criminals, and something like this wouldn't send Eddie to jail for long.

Too bad. Because he deserved that and more.

Isaiah and Leon joined her on the porch a few minutes later. Leon was holding the pizza box and looking at her with a mixture of surprise and admiration. "You arrested my dad."

"Yep. Looks like you'll be staying here for a while until we get that all figured out." She smiled. "Take the pizza into the house and put it in the fridge but avoid the blood stains on the floor. We still have cleaning to do."

Leon nodded and disappeared inside.

"You goaded Leon's dad into taking a swing at you," Isaiah said in a low voice. "My heart just about stopped when he swung that bottle toward your head."

"Who me?" She gave him her best *I'm innocent* look. "I asked him about his son, that's all. He's the one who took offense to the truth."

"Ah, Rae. That's what I love about you." Isaiah swept her into his arms and hugged her tight.

There he went with the L word again. She was about to ask him to clarify what he meant but he captured her mouth in a deep kiss.

Then she decided words weren't necessary.

ISAIAH DIDN'T EVER WANT to stop kissing Raelyn. The immediate danger was over, and he had waited a long time to hold her like this. But they couldn't linger, with Leon inside waiting for them. He kissed her as long as he dared, before lifting his head to gaze down at her. With the arrest of the Chief and hopefully others involved in the scheme, he knew they were blessed to have come out of this situation alive and unharmed.

And most of that was due to her.

"I love you, Raelyn." He'd said it several times now, but she acted as if she hadn't heard him. Probably because he was rushing things just a bit.

Okay, a lot. But he knew his heart, and he wanted her to know that he was serious about this. About making a relationship between them work.

"I—don't understand." His tough, female cop was adorable when she blushed. "Why?"

"I love you because you're strong, sweet, and kind. You are beautiful inside and out." He tucked a strand of her honey-colored hair behind her ear. "You don't hesitate to put your life on the line for others."

"You do those things too," she said in protest. "You're a much better person than I am, Isaiah. I'm only just learning about God and faith. You're here to support the entire community. Taking Leon in without hesitation is proof of that."

"You would have asked me and Leon to come to your place if it hadn't burned down," he said with a smile. "Don't you see? We're alike in so many ways."

"And we're very different too." She frowned.

"I know. And those differences will keep us on our toes." Maybe she couldn't bring herself to put a name to her feelings. And if so, that was okay. He knew she cared for him. The way she'd responded to his kiss gave him hope. No one could fake the chemistry sizzling between them. "Come on. We have work to do."

"Wait." She didn't step out of his arms. "I—what exactly are you saying? That you want to see me again when this is over?"

"Yes, I want that very much. I love you. I care about you, and I want you to be in my life." He wasn't sure how else to say it. "We can take things as slow as you need. I'll understand if you're not ready or feel the same way. I only ask that you give me, give *us* a chance. I know a relationship with me won't always be easy, but you need to know that even if we argue or disagree, I'll never stop loving you."

"Because God brought us together." She smiled, and his heart bloomed with hope as she went up on her tiptoes to kiss him again. "I love you, too, Isaiah. And I have never, ever said those words to anyone else."

"Sweet, Raelyn," he whispered. "I've never been in love like this before either."

She looked uncertain, then shrugged. "I guess we can learn together, then. Because I'm not really sure how this whole love thing works."

He chuckled, lowered his head to kiss her again, but was interrupted by Leon's face at the door.

"Hey, what are you doing out there? I thought we were gonna clean up the place, together."

"We are." He smiled ruefully, gave her another quick kiss, then stepped back. "Okay, Leon. We're coming in to help."

Cleaning the place didn't take as long as he'd expected with the three of them working together. Leon was eager to assist, maybe because of the pizza but more likely because Raelyn had arrested his dad.

Isaiah would apply to become a foster parent so that he could keep Leon with him indefinitely. It would take time for the state to open a case file on Eddie Smith.

He prayed the state would take away Eddie's parental rights without delay. That man wasn't fit to have a pet toad, much less a child.

"Come with me, Leon," Isaiah said when they'd finished. "The bedrooms are upstairs."

Leon's gaze was full of apprehension. He wasn't sure why the boy looked uncomfortable as he led the way up to the second level. He opened the first door on the right, then stepped back. He waved a hand, indicating the boy should go inside. "This will be your room, Leon."

"Really?" Leon's eyes widened in surprise as he gazed around the room. It was nothing fancy—a bed, a dresser, and a nightstand with a lamp. "I get my own bed?"

His blood ran cold. "You don't have your own bed at home?" he asked carefully.

"I sleep on a mattress on the floor in the living room." Leon stepped into the room and ran his hand over the polyester bedspread. "It's nice. And soft."

"Oh, Leon." Raelyn looped her arm around the boy's shoulders and hugged him. "You deserve a room of your own."

"Yes, you do." His voice sounded low and rough with emotion. Rae was her usual amazing self, embracing the boy and soothing his fears.

"Thank you." Leon leaned against Raelyn for a moment, then turned to look at him. "I'm glad to be here."

"We're happy to have you," he assured the boy.

"So—like, are you guys living together?" Leon asked.

Raelyn's cheeks went pink, and he quickly shook his head. "Not the way you're thinking. There was a fire in Raelyn's home, so she needs a place to stay. There are three bedrooms here. I'll show you." He moved out into the hallway and opened the next door on the left. "This is where Raelyn will sleep. And my room is on the end. This is the bathroom." He opened that door too. "We all have to share the bathroom, so keep it clean for Raelyn, got it?"

"Got it," Leon echoed. He still appeared awestruck by having his own room.

The poor kid didn't have anything but the clothes on his back, but he was smiling as they returned downstairs. He ran ahead, asking, "Can we watch TV?"

"Sure. Go ahead." He held back, reaching for Raelyn's hand.

She stood beside him. "I think we need to head to the store tomorrow morning," she murmured. "That poor kid needs clothes that fit him." She turned to look up at him. "And I know you're going to apply to be a foster parent for him, and then will want to adopt him, too, so we should get him a few additional things too."

"Yes, that's exactly what I have planned. Interesting how easily you read my mind." He snuck in another quick kiss. "See how much we think alike? Yet another reason why I love you."

She smiled and shook her head. "You're a goof. But I love you too." She tugged him toward the sofa. "Let's see what Leon has picked out for us to watch, shall we?"

"Why not?" He allowed her to draw him to the sofa. Leon sat on the floor, probably without even noticing the empty stuffed chair next to the couch.

The movie was one he'd never seen, but he couldn't have cared less what Leon wanted to watch. He could gladly sit here and happily gaze at Raelyn for the rest of the evening.

That she understood his need to be there for Leon spoke volumes. Most women would run screaming in the opposite direction, but not Raelyn. She'd stepped up to take on Eddie Smith, tricking him into taking a swing at her.

She knew the importance of providing a stable home

life for Leon. And she would do her part in making that happen.

He needed to convince her that Leon was just the beginning. Together, they could do so much good for the neighborhood.

He swallowed a grin. Despite her misgivings, Raelyn would make a great pastor's wife.

EPILOGUE

Three weeks later . . .

Raelyn had stopped to see what was left of her home, before heading back to Isaiah's. The workers were in the process of removing the charred remnants of the structure. She'd never gone inside to see what she could salvage. There was no point. Her clothing had been damaged by smoke and water.

She turned away, ironically feeling lighter now that she'd made her decision to move on. The insurance company had confirmed the place was a total loss and had offered her a settlement in lieu of rebuilding. She was glad she'd taken the settlement.

She had zero interest in staying in Greenland. In the short time she'd been staying with Isaiah and Leon, she'd grown comfortable in the neighborhood.

Oh, it was still dangerous, but she had noticed that several of the neighbors nodded at her and Isaiah as they worked outside. Leon, too, had blossomed under Isaiah's care. Having a safe place to sleep, three meals a day, and access to the public library had proven to be a boost for Leon, who loved to read.

Not that Leon was perfect, because he wasn't. Isaiah had caught him smoking and nearly blew a gasket. She reminded him that many teenagers experimented with smoking and to be thankful it wasn't pot or something worse.

Then she'd sat Leon down and explained that as a cop, she would have to issue him an underage smoking ticket if he did that again.

Leon had looked at her warily as if trying to judge if she was fibbing or not. Then he shrugged and admitted he hadn't liked smoking much anyway.

Mayor Critten had stepped down from office after his son's arrest. He'd claimed not to know anything about Beau's drug dealing, but in this instance, the truth didn't matter. Perceptions were everything, and it was difficult to portray yourself as someone who would be tough on crime while your son has been arrested for running a drug ring in his old neighborhood.

Hugo Morrison had opened up about his deeds after hearing about Beau's arrest. And injured police officer Brett Carson had identified Reggie as the one who had shot him. Not Pinky.

Additionally, it had only taken Beau two days of being in jail for him to cooperate with the authorities. At least five others were arrested as a result of the information he'd spilled, including Reggie Vallera and, surprisingly, the kid with the street name of Congo. Each one of them were booked for dealing drugs for Beau Critten, on top of other charges related to the original shooting.

It felt good to take down a drug-dealing ring. And she had Isaiah and Leon to thank for the role they had played.

Especially Leon, who had given his statement several times to the authorities without varying a single detail. Obviously, Officer Carson's identifying Reggie as the shooter helped prove Leon's innocence.

She drove to Isaiah's, enjoying the warmer weather. Pulling into the driveway, she saw that both Isaiah and Leon were on the small front lawn tossing a baseball back and forth. She had to grin when she saw Leon's new baseball glove.

"Hey, Rae, guess what?" Leon caught the baseball, then ran toward her. He seemed to have grown a full inch in the past few weeks. He threw his arms around her in an exuberant hug. "I get to stay with Isaiah!"

"Really? That's wonderful!" She gladly hugged him back, meeting Isaiah's warm gaze over his shoulder. She assumed Isaiah's role as church pastor had smoothed the path to become Leon's foster parent. The fact that his father had drugs and tons of empty liquor bottles lying around the house had been enough for the state to sever Eddie's parental rights to the boy.

Especially after Leon had testified to how his father had smashed his pinky with a hammer three years ago. This time, his mother wasn't there to lie for Eddie. Raelyn had tried to find Leon's mother, but so far there was no sign of the woman. She and Isaiah prayed she wasn't dead.

"Yeah." Leon turned back to Isaiah. "I know you want me to practice forgiveness, but I'm glad my dad is still in jail."

"I know." Isaiah squeezed Leon's shoulder. "Practice is the key word. We must try."

"I guess." Leon shrugged, then stepped back to toss the baseball up into the air, catching it with his new mitt. "Can I go hang out with Snoop and Dagger?"

"Sure." Isaiah nodded. "But you know the rules. Be home by dinnertime. And no breaking the law."

"Yeah, yeah." Leon rolled his eyes. "Everyone knows I live with a cop anyways."

"Good. That means they'll be on their best behavior," Isaiah said with satisfaction.

Leon ran off, leaving her alone with Isaiah. He tossed his baseball glove and mitt aside to pull her in for a kiss. "I missed you," he murmured.

"Ditto," she whispered.

After a long, sweet kiss, he lifted his head. "I love you so much."

"I love you too." She wrapped her arms around his neck. "Did you file the paperwork to formally adopt Leon?"

His blue eyes widened. "How did you know?"

"I knew you would sooner or later." She grinned. "You know it won't always be easy."

"From what I hear, even families who live in the nice neighborhoods can have troublesome teens." He grimaced. "Take Petey Dobbs for instance. He had money and died because of his drug addiction. So yeah, I know there will be tough times ahead. I'm ready for that." He hesitated, then asked, "What about you?"

She tipped her head to the side. "I don't know what you mean."

He stepped back and dropped to one knee. "Raelyn, I don't have the money to buy you diamonds, but will you please marry me?"

"Yes, Isaiah. I would be honored to marry you." A pastor's wife. Who would have thought? The guys on the team had given Isaiah the nickname Preacher. "And yes, I know that means Leon would be our son."

"You don't mind?" He rose to his feet, searching her gaze.

"I would mind if we didn't adopt him." She kissed him again. "I love you. Together, we can change our corner of the world."

"With God's strength and love," Isaiah agreed, hugging her close.

For someone who'd never had much of a family, she decided theirs was everything she could have asked for. And more.

I HOPE you enjoyed Raelyn and Isaiah's story in *Raelyn*. I've been having fun bringing love to each member of Rhy's tactical team. Are you ready for Grayson and Eve's story in *Grayson*? Click Here!

and access to a bonus epilogue featuring Elly and Joe's wedding!

Until next time,

Laura Scott

PS: Read on for a sneak peek of *Grayson*.

GRAYSON

Chapter One

Dr. Eve Shaw inwardly sighed as she pulled into the physician parking lot of the Milwaukee College of Medicine located on the same campus as Trinity Medical Center. How embarrassing to be running late to her own presentation. It wasn't Eve's fault—a harried mother of three had rear-ended her near the day care center. The damage to Eve's SUV wasn't bad, the car was drivable, but the young mother had insisted on calling the police to get the accident on record for her insurance company. Why, Eve wasn't sure as most rear-end accidents were the second driver's fault. Maybe she'd feared Eve would come back at her for some reason. A ridiculous notion as she didn't have time for that nonsense.

On a positive note, her presentation was via a live-streaming platform with other molecular cellular researchers, so at least she didn't have to worry about walking in late to a huge auditorium full of medical students and professors waiting for her. She'd already done her grand rounds presentation to them last month. This was a smaller group of professors who would hopefully be understanding over her tardiness. She pushed out of her driver's side door, grabbed her oversized shoulder bag, and squinted against the bright June sun.

As she strode quickly to the Milwaukee College of Medicine's research institute where her office was located, she glanced at her watch. Her presentation was supposed to start right now. She inwardly winced. By the time she got into her office and booted up her computer, she'd be at least seven minutes la—

Boom! A large explosion rocked the earth beneath her feet. Despite her comfy shoes, she was knocked off her feet, her backside hitting the concrete hard enough to make her teeth rattle. Dazed, she looked up at the research building.

Flames and a long plume of black smoke trailed out of one of the office windows. She blinked, trying to compre-hend what had happened.

A gas leak? Had to be. Then she realized the smoke and flames were coming from her office window. Wait. Was that right? She double-checked to be sure, counting the windows. She'd been recently promoted to full professor, which had resulted in a move to a large corner office on the fourth floor.

There was no mistake. It was her office.

"Ma'am, are you okay?" A uniformed officer rushed toward her from a nearby squad, his expression concerned. She stared up at him in confusion, struck off-balance for the second time that day.

"Grayson?" Her voice came out a high squeak.

"Eve? Are you okay?" Grayson Clark loomed over her. Was she imagining things? She hadn't seen the overwhelm-ingly handsome and charismatic Grayson since high school.

They had been lab partners in advanced chemistry. And while they'd both graduated in the same class, he was two years older than she was because she'd graduated from high school at sixteen.

"Yes." She had no clue Grayson had become a cop. "What happened?"

"I'm not sure." He held out his hand, and she allowed him to help her stand. She was annoyed at the tingle of awareness that raced along her nerves. Then she told herself it wasn't him but the shock over what had just transpired. "I was leaving Trinity Medical Center after dropping off a prisoner patient when I saw the explosion."

Shading her eyes with her hand, she looked up at the damaged corner of the building. "That's my office."

"What?" Grayson grasped her arm. "You work in there?"

"Yes, of course." His gaze belatedly dropped to her Milwaukee College of Medicine name badge clipped to her collar. "I'm supposed to be doing a presentation from my office."

Grayson's expression turned grave. "You're saying the bomb was meant for you?"

Her eyes widened as the realization sank deep. "I—well, that seems a bit paranoid, doesn't it? I'm sure it was random, right? I mean, who would want to hurt me?"

"I was hoping you could tell me." Grayson's dark-brown eyes bored into hers. "I see you're a doctor. Is this related to a patient situation? Or something else?"

"I'm not that kind of doctor." She flushed and ran her fingers through her brown hair. It was a nervous habit she'd thought she'd kicked. "I have a PhD in molecular biology." When he frowned, she added, "I'm a research scientist. I've been working for the past five years on a way to rejuvenate pancreatic cells to essentially cure diabetes." A horrible thought struck. "My notes! They're inside my office!"

She tried to pull out of his grasp, but he brought both of his hands up to cup her shoulders. "I'm sorry, Eve, but you can't go in there. Don't you have your notes backed up on the computer system?"

A wave of anguish hit hard. She did have most of her notes on the computer, but not all of them. She doodled when ideas came to her and had many notes lying about on her desk, some she'd stuffed in a file folder.

As she stood there, watching the fire burn in her office, she reminded herself that most of her research was still intact. Whatever ideas she'd jotted down on random sticky notes would come to her again.

Wouldn't they? They'd have to.

She was so close to a breakthrough. She couldn't allow a horrible bomb to set her back.

"Dispatch, this is unit eight. I'm at the scene of an explosion at the Milwaukee College of Medicine. Please send additional units to this location."

Realizing Grayson was right about her inability to go inside, she fished in her large bag for her phone. At the very least, she needed to contact Professor Firestein to tell him she wasn't going to make her presentation.

On cue her phone rang. She pulled it free, and quickly answered, "This is Dr. Shaw."

"You're late," Firestein said irritably.

"I know, there was an explosion in my office." Saying the words was surreal. "I'm afraid we'll have to reschedule."

"Explosion?" Firestein's tone rose in alarm. "What in the world is going on over there?"

That was a really good question. Too bad she didn't have an equally good answer. "I don't know. Might be one of those groups who assume all researchers use stem cells or animals." She didn't use either for her field of study, but it was the only theory she could come up with. "I'm sorry for the inconvenience."

"Oh—ah, don't worry about that." He sounded apologetic now. "I'm just glad you're okay. I'm sure you're right about one of those extremist groups. People have no idea what goes into research like ours. But you can guarantee that if they were struck by illness, cancer, or diabetes, or Alzheimer's, they'd be first in line for the new treatments people like you and I have created for them. I hope the police will do a thorough investigation."

"The police are here, and I'm sure they will. I'll be in touch about rescheduling my presentation for another time." She ended the call, unwilling to discuss the issue further. Dave Firestein was a colleague, but the last thing she needed was for him to tell others about this potential setback. Sometimes researchers could be weirdly competitive about getting their research published in top-notch journals. And her cutting-edge research had many of her colleagues impressed and maybe even a little jealous of her success. Especially since she was the youngest professor on staff.

The shrill sound of fire truck sirens split the air. Grayson still held her arm, and now he nudged her back from the burning building.

"I—don't know what to do." She hadn't felt this discombobulated since she'd entered college at sixteen. The first year had been difficult. After conquering the world of academia, she'd found her place here within the Milwaukee College of Medicine's research institute. She loved nothing more than working in her lab.

How much damage had the lab sustained? Would the

equipment be salvageable? She tried not to dwell on the negative, but it wasn't easy. Years of work would be impacted by this explosion. *Years!*

"Tell me again about this presentation of yours." Grayson stepped in front of her, blocking her view of the fire.

She frowned. Hadn't she already done that? Maybe he hadn't heard her clearly because of the fire truck sirens and commotion going on around them "I'm a molecular biologist. I received a national research grant to fund my project to rejuvenate pancreatic cells in children and young adults to cure diabetes." She waved a hand at the building. "That's my office, and it's close to the lab in the center of the building. My work is important, having the potential to change people's lives for the better. But critical enough to justify something like this? That's difficult to comprehend."

"But what about your presentation?" Grayson pressed. "Tell me more about that."

"I was giving an update on my research to a dozen professors across the Midwest via a live-streaming service. I could explain more, but it's rather technical. I was running late because some woman rear-ended me in front of the day care center..." Her voice trailed off.

If she hadn't been hit by the mother of three, she would have been sitting in her office, smiling into her computer screen, introducing herself to her colleagues at the exact moment of the explosion.

Her knees went weak, and she sagged against Grayson's strong frame as the knowledge sank deep. God had been watching over her today. He had sent that poor mother of three directly into her path at the right moment.

This wasn't just about the loss of her research notes.

The bomb had been planted in her office with the

intent to kill her.

A COLD CHILL snaked down Grayson's spine. Difficult to believe that anyone would try to take out a research scientist, but that's exactly what had happened.

And if not for the fender bender, his former high school classmate Eve Shaw would be dead.

"Grayson?" At the sound of his name, he glanced over to see his immediate boss, Lieutenant Joe Kingsley, jogging toward him, dressed in full tactical gear, the way he was. Joe reported to Captain Rhyland Finnegan, and this type of bombing was exactly the type of case their tactical team would be called in for.

"Joe." Up until January, Joe had been a fellow officer, often taking the lead on various situations, which had helped him get promoted to the rank of lieutenant. Like Rhy, Joe wasn't much on titles but remained focused on getting things done. "You got here fast."

"Rhy is concerned about the bombing." Rhy was their explosive device expert, and he'd been training Grayson to become more well versed in the various devices bad guys used to create death and destruction. "He wants you to stay in the loop on this in case there are more devices. He also has the rest of the team en route so that we can evacuate this building and the others nearby to search for additional bombs."

That suited him just fine. The idea of more devices being planted made him anxious to get to work. But they'd need to wait for the firefighters to get the blaze under control.

"Joe, this is Dr. Eve Shaw." Grayson made the introductions. "It's too early to say for sure that she's the target, but that's her office on fire up there. And she was supposed to be there doing a presentation at the time of the explosion."

Joe's eyebrows hiked up in surprise. "Dr. Shaw, do you have any idea who would do something like this?"

"No. It's got to be one of those extremist groups, though." Eve looked pale and shaky. She had been the smartest kid in their entire high school, having graduated as his class valedictorian with a higher than 4.8 GPA. Grayson wasn't nearly as smart; he would have failed that chemistry class if Eve hadn't been his partner.

"What kind of extremist group?" Joe asked.

"Eve is a molecular biologist. She's doing research on a way to rejuvenate pancreas cells in children and young adults with diabetes, although she doesn't use stem cells or other animal testing. Those types of groups might assume she is, though." He had no clue what that sort of work entailed, but he wasn't surprised by her vocation. Eve had confided in him about her mother's struggles with the disease. He had confidence in Eve's ability to find a cure. "Her office is the source of the explosion. She was supposed to be giving a presentation but was running late. It certainly seems as if she was the target here."

Joe whistled. "Okay, then you need to stick to her like glue until we make sure we have found all the devices."

He nodded grimly. "We need to check her vehicle. And her home."

"The bomb was in my office. I was fine at home this morning," Eve protested.

"The device was planted and detonated according to your schedule," he reminded her. "It's entirely possible that after leaving here, the bomber went to your place to plant another device as a backup." He turned to scan their surroundings, wondering if the bomber was here watching or had already left the scene. He narrowed his gaze on the parking lot. "Which car is yours?"

"The bright-blue SUV." Eve still looked dazed by the near miss. And he didn't blame her. Just the thought of her being killed made his stomach churn.

"Stay here with Joe." He gently pushed her toward his boss. "I'll check it out."

"Do you want backup?" Joe asked with a frown.

"No need. This shouldn't take long." On a cold January night eighteen months ago, their tactical team robot, Dot, had been used to examine a possible explosive device planted in an apartment mailbox. Unfortunately, the device detonated, blowing Dot to pieces. They had a new robot now, Dot version 2.0 named Dottie, that was used by Officer Gully Sullivan, their robot expert. But it would take too long for Dottie to get here, and besides, he was fairly certain he was being paranoid over nothing. If there was a device in her car, it would have detonated in the fender bender.

He crossed the parking lot to Eve's bright-blue SUV. He winced at the color that would stand out from a mile away. Taking his time, he carefully examined the vehicle from a safe distance before moving in closer. Hunkering down, he carefully felt along the wheel wells first, then the bumpers. He noticed the long crack in Eve's rear bumper as he made his way around the vehicle.

When that was completed, he stretched out on his back, pulled a retractable slanted mirror from his pack, sort of a larger version of a dentist instrument, and used that to examine the undercarriage. It was painstaking work because he didn't want to miss anything important.

But after a solid fifteen minutes, he deemed the car to

be clean and safe to use. With relief, he rose to his feet and headed back to where Eve and Joe waited.

"It's fine." He glanced at Joe. "I think we need to take a few teammates with us to sweep her house too."

Eve scowled. "The research building is a public place where anyone can get inside. I keep my house locked when I'm not there."

"Wait a minute, what do you mean the research building is a public place?" Grayson didn't like the sound of that. "Wouldn't your office, and especially the lab itself, be locked?"

"Well, yes, that's true." She nodded, then added, "But the main lobby is open to anyone who wants to come in. Mostly medical students or other adjunct faculty who want to chat with one of us. We're a teaching facility as well as performing research. We have a receptionist who will also schedule meetings for us if necessary." Her eyes widened in alarm. "Do you think Barbra is okay? And what about the other researchers? Had anyone been hurt or..." Again, her voice trailed off.

"It's too early to know," Joe said quietly. "All we can do is pray for the best possible outcome."

Grayson knew Joe, Rhy, and many of their teammates were all believers. At first, he'd been annoyed, not liking the way they'd prayed before eating or discussed various aspects of their faith.

But he'd gotten used to it and had begun to wonder if they were onto something.

"I can't stand it," Eve whispered. "I don't know how I'll live with myself if others died because of me."

"Not because of you, Eve," Grayson hastened to assure her. "Because of the man or woman who planted that bomb. You didn't ask for this."

She bit her lip and shook her head. "I know," she managed. "But still, I want to hear about the conditions of Geoff Abbot and Allan Ballard as soon as possible. They're the two assistant professors with offices closest to mine."

"I'll see what I can do," Joe promised.

Grayson nodded at Joe. "They're going to be tied up here for a while. Let's head over to Eve's house. Make sure the place is clear."

"Okay, what's the address?" Joe asked.

The two men looked at Eve, who quickly answered, "I live close, maybe ten to fifteen minutes away on Maple Creek Parkway." She rattled off the house number.

"Okay, that sounds good." He turned to Joe. "Do you want to come along?"

"Yeah, hang on, we need a couple more people to get this done." Joe lifted his hand to his radio, speaking into it. "I need two officers who are closest to the Maple Creek Parkway to meet me and Grayson at the following address."

Grayson heard the call in his radio, too, quickly followed by a response. "This is Roscoe. I'm almost at the research institute."

"Jina here, I'm en route too."

"Great. Peel off and meet us at the private residence of Dr. Eve Shaw," Joe directed. "Grayson and I will meet up with you shortly."

"Ten-four," Roscoe drawled. Despite being with the team for almost six months, replacing their murdered teammate, Kyle, Roscoe still spoke with his native Texas accent.

"Is this related to the bombing?" Jina asked.

"Affirmative. Details to follow." Joe cut off further communication. "Let's hit the road."

Grayson was glad to be doing something constructive.

"Eve, are you okay to drive? Or do you want to ride with me?"

"I can drive." She still looked pale and shaken, but there was a hint of anger in her stormy gray eyes too.

Oddly, he would have preferred she rode with him. But he forced a nod. "I'll walk you to your car."

She didn't respond but turned and walked back to the bright-blue car. He stayed close, without intruding on her personal space. Obviously, the reality of the situation was still sinking in. Her research and likely others would suffer because of this.

The work of a fanatic as Eve had suggested? Or something more sinister?

"Are you married? Divorced? Seeing anyone?" he asked. Then realizing how that sounded, he quickly added, "Is there a possibility this bomb was planted by someone close to you in a gesture of revenge?"

"You seriously think someone would kill me because I broke off a relationship?" She stopped at her car to look at him skeptically.

"Eve, I'm a cop. I've seen all sorts of personal situations go bad." He thought about the recent attempt to kill Pastor Isaiah Washington and the sex-trafficking ring they'd helped bust up a few months before that. People did horrible things to each other every day. "I know you mentioned fanatic groups who think you're doing research with stem cells or animals, but this could be something personal too."

She stared at him for a long moment, then sighed. "I broke off a relationship with Andrew Thomas three months ago. He's a physician's assistant at Trinity Medical Center." She shrugged. "I'm sure he's moved on to the next woman by now. Monogamy wasn't his strong suit."

"Andrew Thomas," he repeated. "What does a physician's assistant do exactly?"

"He works on the diabetes team. That's how we met." She flushed. "He was really interested in my research, and we started dating. At first it was fun, but I soon realized all he cared about was my work. He—wasn't interested in me as a woman."

Grayson frowned. "That seems strange. You're beautiful and smart. Why wouldn't he be interested in you as a woman?"

Her flush deepened, and she turned away to dig in her bag. "You asked. I'm just telling you that I broke things off, and he was disappointed at first, but he got over it." She opened her car door. "See you soon."

He ruminated over that as he jogged to his squad. He drove up and over the curb to head into the parking lot. There was a rear exit they'd use to leave, as the fire trucks and other emergency rescue personnel were blocking the main road.

Andrew Thomas would have to be checked into. Maybe he had been interested in Eve as a woman, but she hadn't realized it. He'd given her plenty of cues he was interested when they were in high school, but she'd rebuffed him, staring at him intensely through those light-gray eyes of hers before moving on to the next chemistry assignment.

Granted, Eve wasn't really his type. But she was cute in a sexy-librarian type of way. Back then, he'd also dated about half the cheerleaders, so it wasn't as if he'd suffered for female attention.

But that was in the past. He had changed his approach to women since then, keeping them at a distance. But Eve didn't know that.

What difference did it make? He was here to investigate

an attempted murder. He followed her to her small gray brick house where Joe, Roscoe, and Jina were waiting. Her home was small enough that it shouldn't take too long to clear the place.

He quickly joined his teammates and Eve who was handing Joe her keys.

"Eve, will you please wait in your car?" Grayson asked. "Just to be on the safe side?"

She looked as if she might argue but then spun on her heel and returned to her car. Once she slid in behind the wheel, he turned back to the others. "Let's do this."

The four of them approached the house. Once they were inside the living room and kitchen area, they spread out to search.

No surprise, Eve's home was clean and neat. As predicted, it didn't take long to clear the main living space. There were only two bedrooms and a full basement. One bedroom was an office, the other her master suite. "I'll take the office," Grayson offered.

"Jina, take the garage, then join me in the basement. Roscoe, clear the master bedroom and bath," Joe said.

He entered the office, noting with amusement that this space was not neat and tidy. Eve had papers everywhere and a dozen sticky notes pressed on various surfaces. Thinking of her office at the research institute, he approached the desk first. He pulled the chair out and bent to look underneath.

And froze.

A pipe bomb was strapped beneath the desk.

He quickly used his radio to alert the others. "Device found in the office. Evacuate the area ASAP!" Then he took a deep breath and began to slowly back out of the room, anxious to get out of there before it detonated.